First Sight

The Deal Prequel

~

Deborah Ann

Copyright

~

~

Destiny Publishing-Hester
P.O. Box 494661, Redding, Calif. 96049

~

First Published eBook Edition, September 2015
First Published Paperback Edition, September2015

~

~

ISBN 13: 978-0-9967804-1-4 (Paperback Print Edition)
ISBN 10: 0996780416

Dedication

~

To my family, friends, and readers,
with gratitude for their support...

Acknowledgments

~

As always, a big thank you to Brittany for assisting in the cover design. XX ~ A special thank you to Danielle, @lovedaniellesescape, my dear friend and willing supporter, for encouraging me along in my journey. I will forever be grateful. Thank you. OO ~ And to the bloggers, friends and group members I've met along the way, helping to pass the word, I can't thank you all enough. Your support means the world to me. ☺

CONTENTS

~

We tire of those pleasures we take,

but never of those we give. …

~

John Petit-Senn

Chapter One

"Okay, smooches buttercup!" chimed my best friend, Lizzy, leaning over the center console with an air kiss to each of my cheeks. "Rock those Toronto executives with our mad designs and killer ad plan, and show 'em how us kickass California girls do it! Knock their socks off, sweets."

"Will do, partner." I gave her a cheeky grin and squeezed her hand. "I'll see you tomorrow night." I gathered my briefcase, purse and carryon luggage, and popped the passenger door open, ready to embark into the crazy that was Los Angeles International Airport—better known as LAX.

"And while you're at it…maybe you can rock one of those, too," she dramatically nudged her head forward, "*him*, and get yourself out of this slump you're in."

I followed Lizzy's glinting green eyes to the front windshield and out over the hood of her family van, gazing at a black limousine parked in front of us and the gorgeous man who'd unloaded from it, waiting for his chauffeur to collect his travel bags for him. Even from only the side view I had of him, he looked pretty damn impressive: his dark hair, not a tousled strand out of sorts or looking anything but perfect; his skin was beautifully tanned with a classic California glow, giving me the impression he was a local man; his jawline was softly chiseled, and his frame... *Wow!* ...he seemed to be muscular and had the advantage of height; his steely blue suit stretched over his broad shoulders, lending a glorious hint at the muscles that lay beneath, and his suit slacks fit snug on his thick, muscular thighs. *He was well-built, and impeccably dressed.* His profile was perfect! I only wished I could see his eyes; I imagined they were just as dreamy as the rest of him.

He buttoned his perfectly tailored suit jacket and smoothed his hands over the front of it, straightening it out and assuring his perfection before he made his grand entrance into the busy airport terminal. (It wasn't necessary; he was pretty well darn near perfect already.) My heart skipped and paused a beat, waiting for the lovely long legs of a beautiful woman to follow him out of the open car door. But, to my surprise, one never followed.

As if willing him to, the man turned with a brief, casual glance our way. *Those lips.* Holy mother of Christ! The man was *hot.* Though, I didn't say as much to Lizzy. No, I said, "Humph! A wealthy, pompous control freak businessman who disarmingly flits from one shattered female heart to the next... No thank you!" I vowed. "He wouldn't want a girl like me, anyway." *Besides, I'm sworn off men...*

Incredulous, Lizzy swung her gaze back to me. "What...smart, strong, successful, *and* beautiful? No, totally unappealing to men." She shook her head at me. "That type of man is exactly what you need to shake it up. It's been two months since you broke it off with dipshit Brian; I'm assuming you've been with no one since?"

Ugh! I swung my legs out of the open car door, remembering we were parked in a drop off *only* zone, curbside. "Gotta go! Thanks for the lift." *Yeah, I'll be taking a cab home from the airport upon my return.* I bent down and looked back at Lizzy, blowing her a goodbye kiss.

To which Lizzy replied, "One night stand, baby!" giggling as I shut the car door and turned my back on her, my high heels at a fast pace into the terminal. *Most definitely taking a cab on my return route!*

The thought was absurd; I don't do one night stands. EVER! And now's not the time to start. I'm a twenty-eight year old woman, not a college co-ed call-me-for-a-good-time party girl. I shook the ridiculous image from my mind and set after locating my boarding gate. I briefly considered stopping into the luxury pre-boarding lounge for a stiff drink or shot…or two or three. But thought better of it—arriving in Toronto plastered would not be ideal. Nor would alerting Homeland Security to my inebriated self and being frisked like a threat or terrorist to the country before being allowed to board… Or worse, being *disallowed* to board…

As typical, my flight was running late—fog or something over San Francisco. I decided to make a trip to the restroom to freshen up a bit before the nearly five hour long flight, to avoid the need on board, and possibly relieve a little of this anxiety, as well.

My hands bracing me on a section of the sink counter, I leaned over one of the bathroom sinks, staring at my reflection in the mirror, the thought of a one night stand rolling around in my head… *Could I do it? A one night stand? If it were a man like Mr. Devastatingly Gorgeous from the limo…?* Hmm. My body tingled head to toe, a delicious shiver traveling down my spine, sparking my inner parts alive and sending a delightful warmth passing through me—

I was abruptly shaken out of my reverie, "Now boarding flight AC790 to Toronto Pearson International Airport," coming over the PA system and echoing throughout the oversized restroom. *Good God*, what had Lizzy done to me? I shook the dreamy thoughts from my head. *I'm traveling on business!* And just like that, I snapped my focus back to the mission at hand—blowing the minds of the CEO and board of executives for *The Grand International Concierge Hotel and Suites* chain with our kickass design and advertising plan, smearing my competition and landing the account—as I darted off toward my flight.

As I approached my first class seat and settled my slim, five foot ten frame in, I was pleased to see the seat beside me was empty. *What are the chances I'd be seated alone for the duration of the flight?* I wondered briefly as we were alerted to fasten our seatbelts. I did as asked and buckled up, just as Mr. Gorgeous

Limousine Man, all cool and calm, swept up to the seat beside me. *Jesus*, the man smelled good—a mix of fresh, clean, spicy, masculine, oozing sex appeal, man. *Intoxicating man!*

I held my breath and turned my pale blue gaze to the window. This was going to be a very long flight seated beside Mr. Smell Good Drop Dead Gorgeous, intoxicating me and seducing me with his sexy man mojo.

He hoisted his carryon up with one hand and slipped it into the overhead compartment. I felt his height hovering beside me. *Holy cow he was tall. At least six foot five.* I was suddenly smacked with a vision of those sexy, long, muscular legs wrapped around me… horizontally… pressed against me… between me… beneath me… *Oh my*, Lizzy and her damn suggestion of a one night stand.

Mr. Gorgeous oozed his yummy self into the seat beside me, setting his laptop case on the floor between the toes of his fancy, Italian shoes and sliding it under the chair in front of him, just as I had mine. His seatbelt was then buckled, ready for takeoff.

I darted my eyes back to the window, pretending to have not noticed him—or the long, thick fingers that had just caressed his seatbelt while buckling it, never before more envious of an inanimate object in my life—acting completely unaffected and uninterested.

"Hello," came the sexiest voice I'd ever heard, smooth and deep, seeming to speak directly to a bundle of secret places within me. *Heavens*. I slowly turned back, giving him a glance.

The word 'breathtaking' came to mind.

Had I ever *seen* a breathtaking man before?

Certainly not one such as him. The word was created for him …Had been *inspired* by him.

He hit me with a million dollar smile, all big, brilliant and bright white. *Damn if it wasn't swoon worthy.* Then he stunned me with his gaze, drawn there as his smile reached at the corners, crinkling just the slightest. I found myself looking into the most mesmerizing pale blue-green eyes I'd ever seen, absolutely striking in contrast to his dark hair. *Bedroom eyes*, that's what they were. *Another damn swoon worthy feature.*

I was captivated right away, and under his spell. His hand

politely came toward me, "Adam Blaire." I was speechless as he took my hand in his and placed a light kiss on the back, his thumb lightly stroking my fingers. Those blue-green bedroom eyes looked up at me through thick dark lashes, "And you are?"

"Ah...uh, um—" And now I was a blubbering idiot, fool, tongue all tied up. *Holy hell*. He hit me with the smile again. And what the heck was that, with his touch? It felt like sparks striking out against my palm and zinging through me. Like a thrilling bolt of lightning, rousingly nestling smack-dab between my legs.

Damn, what'd he say his name was again?

He let go of my hand and I tucked it into my side, under my other arm, subtly wiping the sweat from my palm. I closed my eyes and tried to find my center...or at least summon my wits to return. Jeez. And what the hell, *sweaty palms*? What was I, sixteen?

I felt the force of the pressure in the cabin upon take off, our plane readily ascending into the sky. I let out a large breath of air, and quickly took in another. *Phew*. That seemed to help. Feeling more myself, I pushed out with the next breath, "Bethany..." Well, that was something; at least I remembered my *own* name.

"Delighted to meet you, Bethany." His lips curled into an amused grin. "Not a fan of flying, I take it?"

Oh God, it had nothing to do with the flying, but I wasn't about to tell him that. It was better that he thought I was a nervous flyer. So I just gave him a weak smile.

I was relieved when the plane leveled off and I saw our cabin attendant flittering about.

A drink, that's what I needed—not that sitting beside this man for the next few hours wouldn't be intoxicating enough. *Mercy.* He should come with a warning label. ~ *Danger! Hazardous to the heart and senses of all women, and possibly men, sensible or otherwise. Likely to cause extreme levels of inebriation.* ~

I should have had that drink-*slash*-shot in the pre-boarding lounge after all...screw Homeland Security.

Get a grip Bethany. The man has trouble written all over him —the delicious kind of trouble—and you're sworn off men. Likely for good!

His unbelievable eyes locked on mine. "What has you traveling today, Bethany? Meeting up with your boyfriend, perhaps?"

Ah, clever man. Hinting around the boyfriend topic. "No. Business."

"And you left your boyfriend behind," he pushed, "fervently awaiting your return?"

Okay; now he was just annoying me. Whether or not I had a boyfriend was none of his concern. And was altogether too forward, seeing as he'd only just sat down beside me.

He leaned in a little closer, intoxicating me further, and huskily murmured, "If you were mine, I'd never send you off alone. In fact...I'd never let you out of my sight."

His?!

Why did just the thought do unspeakable things to me?

"What about you, Mr. Wealthy Limo Man?"

His brows furrowed. "How'd you know I arrived in a limousine?"

Oh crap.

"Lucky guess... You looked the type."

"Oh?" He pulled back. "And what type is that, exactly?"

I cocked my head to one side with a knowing expression. "A convenient business trip; break from the wife and kids?"

He choked and coughed in combination with a sputtery chuckle. "Bite your tongue, sweetheart!

I giggled. "Okay. So no kids yet? Just a trophy wife?" This guy was kind of fun.

He looked a little amused, by the crooked grin toying at one corner of his mouth. "You've got me pegged all wrong, beautiful."

"Oh, how so?" I played along, trying not to get swept up in the fact that he'd called me beautiful, and seemed to be flirting with me. *Me*!

"No kids, no trophy wife, and no girlfriend." He dipped down and quickly snatched his laptop from under the seat in front of him, and then straightened up in his seat, turning the full wattage of his smile and power of his gaze on me. *Wow*. "Other than a high school girlfriend that I ended things with in law school, I've never even come close..." he paused, "to, eh, locking it down, so to speak. I'm a divorce attorney. I've yet to see one that has worked out; whether it marriage, or a relationship."

"Hmm. So you're a wealthy playboy?"

"Back to you; boyfriend? I see no ring, so no lucky man's claimed you as his wife?"

Claimed me? "If you must know, I'm recently sworn off men."

Incredulous, he said, "Why would you do such a thing? Clearly, men must fall at your feet and worship the very ground you walk on. You hold all the cards, honey. You could demand anything you want, and us poor men would submit willingly to a woman such as yourself."

Ha! Someone forgot to give that memo to my ex. "Yes, so much so that my last boyfriend sought out someone else." Cheating snake in the grass bastard.

"An idiot, that one."

That brought a faint smile to my face. The man was not only gorgeous and yummy smelling, he was charming as well... Disarmingly so.

"Was it serious?"

"Lived together." I squirmed in my seat. This was not a topic I wanted to revisit. Lizzy's reminder in the car was enough. I unconsciously worried one side of my lower lip, crossing and uncrossing my legs.

"He didn't deserve you."

How could he tell? Though true. Too bad I didn't realize that in the first place. I had a bizarre knack for always picking the wrong men.

"Hence why I'm sworn off men; I don't need the distraction or the headache." Nor the heartache, for that matter.

"What a shame," Adam tisked, shaking his head. He set his large hand on the top of my bare thigh, just above my knee. *Whoa*! "Maybe I can persuade you otherwise." His glittering eyes intently gazed into mine, seeking permission before he presumptuously moved his hand any further.

As far as I knew, I gave no indication of consent—ambivalent and *stunned* as I was—but Adam must have seen a flicker of something, because his hand began ascending on a delicious trail up the inside of my bare thigh, his smooth hand slowly gliding along my skin and creeping up under my skirt.

Holy cow! My breath halted in my chest, Adam's eyes never leaving mine.

His other hand gently tugged the inside of my knee, encouraging my legs to part.

Oh. My. God. This was really happening. Here. Now. *In an air cabin of people.* And I was letting it happen; allowing this intimate moment to play out with this complete stranger.

Oddly enough, Adam didn't *feel* like a complete stranger, exactly. He compelled a trust in him that I couldn't deny. Nor did I want to. In some way, I needed this, needed to let it play out. Trust what Adam was giving. And he knew it.

Lizzy's words suddenly rang out in my head, "*That type of man is exactly what you need to shake it up.*" As much as I didn't want to admit it, it seemed she was right… And this was certainly shaking it up in a very bold and brazen way. Shaking in unfamiliar territory. Forbidden territory! And my need for it was strong.

I worked my bottom lip between my teeth as I slid my hand toward him, feeling my way under his laptop and settling between his legs, on his obvious excitement. My frisky fingers gripped around him, but were instantly warned off with the stern shake of his head.

My eyebrows pushed together in frustration, not a bit happy that he was not going to let me reciprocate the gesture of pleasure. I submissively slipped my hand back to the armrest between us, matching the grip my other hand had on the armrest at my other side.

I felt his fingertips whisper against the flesh at the uppermost inside part of my thigh, nearly ready to explode from the heat of his touch so dangerously close, and grinned internally, waiting for him to realize the naughty little surprise that awaited him.

"*Mmmm,*" I softly moaned, in the same moment a low groan escaped from deep within Adam's chest, and there it was—

"Oh, Bethany…Sweetheart…" His face split with a devilish, sexy grin, watching my expression as his body pressed into mine and he did a little shifting of his laptop, shielding view in the close proximity of that cabin before his sinfully wicked fingers explored my pantieless pleasure point; the tip of one finger slipping inside and curling in deep, where my body ached to feel his touch, two more quickly following while his thumb gently pressed and swirled on just the right spot. *Uhh*! I threw my head back against the headrest, my body already trembling. *Oh hell*, I was going to scream out my pleasure, uncontrollably. I bit my lip harder, hoping to hold back my cry.

But suddenly, all concern faded away, Adam's magic fingers inducing a binding peak of pleasure, rapidly cumulating low in my belly and tugging at my center: the slipping, the thrusting, the swirling of those glorious, sinfully wicked fingers... I couldn't take it any longer. *What the hell was he doing to me; never had I felt such need, such carnal desire?* My entire body tensed, my lower half arching into his hand, the slight turbulence adding to my pleasure. A whimper spontaneously escaped between my parted lips, and Adam's mouth at once pressed hard on mine, my release ripping through me like never before, over and over, trembling, quivering, such utter pleasure, as his tongue plunged in, tangling deep with mine and swallowing my cry of pleasure.

Adam's movements slowed, aware of the heightened sensitivity of my delicate, aroused flesh, those magic fingertips gently pressing against the residual throbbing, inducing every last wave of breathtaking pleasure.

Oh. My. Heavens.

Adam's kiss softened, one hand reaching to cup the back of my jaw as he sensuously sucked and drew my lower lip into his mouth, encouraging the throbbing below to persist that much longer, sucking in rhythm.

I clasped a hand at the back of Adam's neck, holding him to me.

Mercy, the man knew what he was doing.

Our location suddenly whirled into thought, and the reality that I was melted into a pool of sensual bliss in my seat. Where the hell had that flight attendant been all this time? I felt like I'd been lost with Adam for hours, oblivious to her frequently passing by.

"Still sworn off men?" came throatily from Adam.

Oh my. That thought couldn't be further from my mind at the moment

Chapter Two

Adam glimmered with a haughty grin, his lustful sea blue eyes gazing upon me, my skin glistening and my body spent, melted into the seat in the afterglow. "That was…"

"Sinful," I filled in for him.

"Spectacular," he countered in a husky, desire wrecked tone as he leaned a little closer, murmuring into my ear, "And choosing to wear no panties today…*hot*!"

Oh my, that didn't even begin to cover it. I was ready to straddle his lap right then and there—regardless of the scene it would stir.

"I need more of you."

What?! Did he *too* want me to straddle his lap?

Wait? How'd he do that, steal my thought and voice it?

Another command hit my ear. "Stay with me."

Absolutely not!

"Let me taste you? All of you."

Ooh. I pressed my thighs together.

Adam's glistening, still moist fingers lifted in to the air and hovered between us, slowly gliding closer.

Don't do it, the voice in my head screamed, *don't do what I've read in those romance novels, bring those sinful fingers to your mouth, or God forbid, mine, with my own arousal…*

Just in case… "I need to, uh, freshen up a minute—"

"I'll help you," Adam was eager to respond, those fingers softly sliding between mine, possessively holding my hand.

Whoa. There were those sparks again.

"I can manage on my own, Mr. Blaire." *Mr. Magic Fingers was more like it.*

But the words had no sooner passed between my lips, when I rose from my seat, and my weak knees gave way and I teetered into Adam's lap. His firm hands gripped my hips. "Sit!" he demanded. "Or I'm going with you!" He wiggled a brow playfully.

Sitting sounded like a fine idea.

Besides, by the feel of Adam's lap, he should have let me reciprocate the pleasure earlier; he was in no condition to be up and walking about, and I was sure my rear rubbing against him wasn't relieving the situation any.

His palms briefly traced the curve of my hips, eyes lustful, before guiding me back into my seat.

The man's hands felt like *fire* against my skin, sending a flood of flaming hot desire rushing through my veins straight to my center.

"I'd prefer you not wash away that scent anyway," he murmured down low.

Jesus Christ!

"It's sexy as hell. Heady—" Adam's breathy words continued to fall over me, caressing my skin as they passed. "Sinfully sweet like no other…"

I blinked up at him, not believing what I was hearing.

"You intoxicate me, sweetheart."

I intoxicate *him*? I was certain that was the other way around.

Our flight attendant made a sudden appearance. "Can I get either of you a beverage?" Her round, brown eyes were glued to Adam.

Not that I could blame her.

"We'll each have a glass of wine, please," Adam answered.

What the heck? So now he was ordering for me? "White for me, please," I asserted. *Adam certainly was a take charge guy*, I was thinking as the attendant shuffled off with her blush tinted cheeks.

"Are you aware what a pair of heels like that does to a man…?" *Huh?* Adam's eyes traveled down the length of my legs and settled on my crimson, high-heeled slingbacks.

The man just oozed sexy; he couldn't even help it.

"I'll give you a moment to think," he rasped. Then he slid his hand from mine. I sat there stunned while he opened up his laptop and got down to business.

Stay with him? Taste me? The thought alone nearly undid me. The visual elicited… I suddenly found myself wondering what Adam would look like naked… While tasting me… That mouth and that tongue… Those long, lean, strong muscles beneath that layer of tanned skin… Beneath *me*… I mentally chided myself— *Work! Business!* The real reason for traveling today. Not a hookup with a stranger—though, beautiful as he was. Sheesh!

I gathered my long, dark hair to one side, draping it over my shoulder as I tilted my legs to the side and reached under the seat in front of me, retrieving my laptop. Time to get back to work. Lizzy and I had been trying to land *The Grand International Concierge Hotel and Suites* account for a month: phone calls back and forth, consulting, emailing, gathering all the necessary facts, needs, and wants to draw our design ideas for the presentation. It's all led to this meeting tomorrow, to determine our place-*slash*-fate with the company.

Work? I shook my head. How was I supposed to work with Mr. Smell Good intoxicating my air? Not to mention all his dirty talk squirming around in my head and scrambling my good sense? Oh, and the big surprise…that I *liked* it, the words he spoke, the sexy sound of his voice…it was completely hot!

I glanced at him, seemingly unaware of his effect, at the same moment catching the woman seated directly across the aisle from Adam, staring at him with a dreamy smile. *Yeah. You and me both, Lady; I'm right there with you.* In a blink her eyes darted to me with a daggered glare. I sucked in a sharp intake of breath. *What the heck did I do to deserve that?*

Adam gave me a sideways glance, with a quizzical look. "Everything all right, Bethany?" I briefly wondered if my expression held the same dreamy smile as Miss Infatuated across the aisle?

Damn sexy man mojo.

I nodded, assuring Adam that I was indeed just fine.

He wasn't appeased, and gently closed his laptop, effectively putting an end to his work.

He reached for my hand, his attention now focused on *me*.

It was a little too close for comfort, for me, and I tensed under the stain of awkwardness, itching to pull my hand from Adam's.

I didn't, of course.

"You have an admirer," I whispered, subtly gesturing toward the glaring woman with my eyes.

Adam placed a kiss on the back of my hand, and then turned to the woman and flashed his panty dropping smile. "I know," he cooed, "isn't she lovely, I can't seem to take my eyes off of her either." Oh my. I hadn't expected that kind of reaction from him. What the heck…?

Stunned, the lady batted her lashes and dropped her gaze.

Well then, maybe he did know his effect. He handled her magnificently.

~ * ~

We'd finished taxiing and were prepared to disembark. With my laptop and handbag gathered in my arms, a movie and a nap under my belt, I was ready to at last hop to my feet and snatch up my carryon. Thanks to the blissful release Adam had so wonderfully blessed me with, along with relieving a month load of bound up tension, I was relaxed enough to doze off for the last portion of the flight. Now I was full of energy and desperate to get moving. Adam had been his charming self for the majority of the flight, but for some reason had been uncharacteristically quiet for the last twenty or so minutes.

I wasn't sure, but I had a little niggle of a thought to why. I took one more look out the window at the expanse of tarmac and uneven rows of parked airplanes, my eyes settling on the baggage handlers. A woman and two men, each dressed in bland, charcoal gray coveralls and a neon yellow vest, were hustling about to get our baggage unloaded from the underbelly of the plane to several small trailers, for transporting.

Adam leaned closer, "Stay with me tonight," he whispered into my ear. "I have a luxury suite, and a car waiting to drive us."

Whoa! The reason to why he'd been so quiet; preparing to stun me with the full power of his persuasive charm. "I have a room. Thank you very much." The closeness of his body pressed to mine, his breath lingering over the delicate flesh of my neck, sent the most delicious shiver tingling down my spine, feeling as if it was whispering up the insides of my thighs and curling at my center.

Lord, this man was magic.

At last time to unload, I hopped to my feet and Adam followed, set to slip our carry-ons from the overhead compartment. Only glaring lady from across the aisle had the same idea and Adam politely let her go first, while we stood waiting.

Adam's one arm fixed around my waist from behind, and he took in the scent of my hair. "Don't tell me you are not willing to explore this? Just one night. Please, sweetheart?" His fingertip swept lightly down my arm and back up, eliciting goose bumps to prickle up on my skin. "Don't leave me with just a taste... wanting—"

"You're...You're a stranger," I stammered, turning to face him. "I don't typically go around picking up strange men in airplanes and letting them take me to their secluded hotel rooms."

"Ouch." He put a hand over his heart, feigning wounded. "I would hope not. But I'm not a stranger...not after... Ask me anything? Anything you want to know."

Oh, there were so many questions... so much I wanted to know... But out came, "When was the last intimate moment you shared with a woman?"

A sexy smirk crept across his face, and his eyes twinkled.

Yeah, just as I thought. I'd be one in a string of woman... No thank you.

"You," he glanced at his expensive watch, "about three hours and twelve minutes ago, right here in these seats."

Oh Lord. I lifted a brow at him, my cheeks flushed with heat. *I swore off men for a reason, damn it, because I'm incapable of choosing properly—and here I am. I'm a magnet for the wrong men!*

He chuckled. "Roughly thirty-two hours ago."

Seriously? Mm mm. No way!

Adam swooped in with an urgent kiss, his tongue intimately dancing with mine and exploring the passionate depths, like it was the last kiss we'd share. The last time his lips would touch my lips. Or, just plain trying to persuade me.

It worked. "Okay," I breathed. *Disarming damn man.* What the heck was I doing?

This was not me, agreeing to such a thing.

I blame it on Lizzy.

This was her fault!

Adam's finger trailed up my spine, his lips leaving a sweet kiss on my cheek.

But, truth was, as much as I wanted to deny it—put blame on Adam's persuasive charm, or Lizzy's power of suggestion—really, I was okay with it; I was ready to take a chance. Ready to feel those passionate lips and strong, skilled hands on the rest of me; ready to explore this intense electricity sparking and tingling between us. The undeniable sexual tension. After all, it's just one night. I'll never see the man again. Los Angeles is a big county, the likelihood of our paths crossing, of us running into one another once we get home, is nearly impossible. Nonexistent. And it's not like I'm going to divulge my full name, where I work, personal details, or give him my contact information. I'm just going to share my body, briefly, for one night. Indulge in a little shared pleasure with an incredibly hot, devastatingly gorgeous man...

Adam slipped our carryon bags from the overhead compartment, and we strolled on our way...

~ * ~

As Adam had said, a town car awaited us curbside on our exit from Toronto Pearson International Airport, the driver standing alongside the back passenger door in a formal stance. Adam handed our bags off to the driver, and with his palm nestled at the small of my back, Adam guided me into the car before him. He climbed in beside me, a wicked grin in place and an electrifying thrill radiating off his body and penetrating into to mine.

My pulse raced in anticipation, adrenaline pumping swift in my veins and white hot desire swirling in my belly.

Adam's palm found my knee as he slid closer, intruding right on into my personal space, his pant leg brushing my bared thigh —the exposed skin below the hemline of my skirt—delicious texture against my sensitive skin. He unexpectedly dropped a light kiss on my cheekbone, murmuring, "Thank you, for agree-ing."

Sheesh, the way the man moved from smokin' hot sexy to honey sweet, had my head in a spin and my insides all aflutter.

My thighs clenched together.

Adam chuckled. "What's the matter, Bethany? Have a little *itch* that needs scratching?" he teased, his fingertips tickling up my thigh and toying with the hem of my skirt.

As a matter-of-fact—

He leaned closer. "Oh, the things I'm going to do to you."

All the air left my lungs.

"You'll never be the same, once I'm through with you, baby."

Adam's lips touched to the curl of my ear, his tongue tracing a moist trail to my earlobe. He gently sucked my earlobe into his mouth, and, "*Mmmmm*," I moaned softly.

"But for now," he nipped at my earlobe and haughtily laughed, "maybe we should talk, for a bit of a distraction."

Yeah. A distraction. That would be nice. *Christ, it was getting hot in this car*. I tipped my head back against the seat with a sigh.

Adam's lips left my earlobe and he moved back, the cool air hitting my wet lobe and sending a tingling shiver coursing deli-ciously down my spine.

"So what's the nature of the business that brought you to Toronto?" he casually asked. "And what is the duration of your stay?" His fingers sashayed past the hemline of my skirt, the tip of one frisky finger quickly swiping between my legs and then vanishing, skimming over my shirt and stealing a feel of my breast.

I slouched into the seat. *I don't think I've ever been breathless without being kissed.*

One arm scooped under my knees and lifted my legs to his lap, a hand settled on the top of my ankles. The other arm lay over my legs, his hand resting on the outside of my thigh, with his fingertips sweeping lightly along my skin.

I sat there staring at him, fire building inside.

"Uh, maybe you shouldn't touch me."

Adam's hands were at once off of me, his palms held up in surrender.

I slipped my legs from his lap and straightened myself into an upright sitting position.

Adam looked at me expectantly. "I asked you a question, Bethany."

Um…What was the question again?

"Have you forgotten what I asked?"

"Of course not." I nonchalantly glanced down and unrumpled my skirt, smoothing my hands over the fabric and picking at imaginary lint. *It was far better than looking into those expectant eyes, while I fibbed.*

I heard another chuckle beside me. "Well, just in case… I asked you what business brought you to Toronto, and how long you plan to stay?"

Yes! That was it. Sheesh, the man could muddle the mind. "I have a meeting with the CEO and top executives for a Toronto based hotel chain. I'm pitching our design ideas for a new worldwide advertising plan, including updating their branding and their website."

Adam raised a questioning brow; which I read as, '*How did you get noticed from LA?*'

"My Company was recommended by another client," I explained. "An LA based client, with Toronto roots."

Adam nodded his head in understanding. "I'm impressed." He ran his fingertip lightly down my neck, from the back of my jaw down along my collarbone. "I appreciate a smart, successful business woman," he murmured in a husky tone. "I find it sexy as hell."

Oh wow.

"Strong, smart, *and* beautiful…?"

I slightly smiled, pressing my lips together to hold back the large grin threatening to force its way out.

If I land this account, it will be a huge boon for my company.

"Which hotel line?" Adam fired out.

I glanced out the car window, deterring my gaze from Adam and giving out nothing.

Adam clasped his hand to the inside of my thigh, sending a jolt of desire shooting through me. "You're really not going to share any personal information or details with me?"

I turned back to him and softly shook my head. "Nope." Just my body, Mr. Blaire.

Adam nodded in acquiescence. "Okay. I see how it is." His fingers inched up my inner thigh, threatening to tease it out of me. "No last name...no business name...no—"

"Stop that!" I slapped his hand away.

"Well, I'm an open book, sweetheart."

Of course he was. Because, unlike a woman, his heart's not involved. He probably had no issue disregarding the throngs of women falling all over him and pursuing him. And most likely did this sort of thing all the time. *Well*, I mused, *I'm taking that cue, and leaving my heart out of it. A one night hookup. That's it.*

I heard the faint sound of "You've got a friend" filling my ears and intruding in my musings. "*Oh, no*," I muttered under my breath, *I forgot to call Lizzy*. I snatched my cell phone from the inside pocket of my handbag and swiftly answered the call. "Hello, Lizzy—"

"'Hello, Lizzy!' That's what you have to say?!" she screeched into my ear. "How about 'I'm sorry, Lizzy!'" *Yikes.* "You were supposed to call when you landed, Beth, to let me know you arrived safely!"

I know, I know. "I'm so sorry, Lizzy. Something, eh, came up."

"What? What came up? Are you all right?!" she rambled in a panicked rush.

"Yes."

"I double checked your reservation, and everything's set."

Ugh. *Perfect.* "There's been a change of plans." I winced. "I'm actually staying at a different hotel. I, uh, can't explain right now...now's not a good time. I'm on the way there."

Adam smirked beside me.

"But everything's fine, Lizzy, no need to worry," I assured her. "I'll call you after I present tomorrow."

"Fine?" Adam mouthed, his lips in a somewhat angry line, insulted at the inadequate, lacking description I'd chosen to describe how things were at the moment. He leaned in... *Holy shit the man was dangerously daunting*. Next thing I knew, he'd slid his hand under my rear and slipped me to my back on the seat, his large, intimidating body looming over me, murmuring, "Maybe I need to rectify that?" He nipped along my jawline.

"I, ah, gotta go Liz—" Adam plucked the phone from my hand and abruptly ended Lizzy's call, tossing the phone onto the floor of the car.

How things were in that moment, truly, were HOT! Though I didn't dare tell Lizzy that; not in front Adam, Mr. Sinfully Sexy.

His lips were on mine and his hand slipped inside the top of my blouse, skimming the lacy edge of my bra. "Who's Lizzy?"

Ahh... He wants to know *now*? While his lips and hands were seemingly touching and stimulating everywhere on my body? "Later," I moaned, my hands clawing at the back of his dress shirt. I felt my skirt whisper up and gather around my waist. My knee touched my chest.

He owned me with his kiss, long and divinely deep and consuming, feeding my need but eliciting another, deeper, in the depths of the sweet, increasingly moist, yummy spaces within. "*Ohhh*." Sweet Lord. Adam's hips pressed against mine, aware of what he was doing to me, the evidence of his desire deliciously rubbing firm on my own, clearly just as affected. I swung my legs around him, hooking my feet on his backside, on the glorious curve of his ass as I squirmed beneath him, separated only by the thin fabric of his slacks and zipper teeth.

"Still just doing *fine*?" he murmured deep and sexy, surprising me with the sudden thrust of his hips.

Oooh.

Heaven have mercy.

He bit my lower lip and then set his tongue on a searing trail over my chin, down my neck and chest and plunging into my cleavage—not the largest valley, but ample enough—nipping and licking at the naked flesh beneath lace.

"No, not, f—fine," I stuttered. Adam's lips locked on the swell of one breast, sucking so hard I felt the tiny cluster of bundled nerves below his grinding hips bind and twist that much tighter, signaling my impending release. "Fan...tastic," I moaned, followed by a whimper. Hell—*a whimper?*—I never whimpered. At least there'd been no whimpering in my past sexual encounters. *Hmm...* I had no time to ponder that thought, my body suddenly quivering, beginning to come undone—

"Mr. Blaire," the voice of our driver suddenly sobered the moment, "We have arrived at your destination, sir."

Adam grumbled, and groaned out, "Thank you, Josh," before biting a nipple though my shirt, and then lifting his head and catching my eyes. "To be continued, sweetheart." He pushed himself off of me and was seated before I got my wits about me, his hands raking through his sexily tousled dark hair and fingering it into place. *Personally, the sexily tousled, works for me.*

Holy hell! I was sprawled out on the backseat, visibly in no condition to exit the back of this car and stroll into an extravagant, luxury hotel.

Adam gave me a wolfish gaze, and then shook his head slowly. "Unless you want me to finish what I started, you better straighten up. Move it. Chop, chop!"

Sheesh, bossy!

He shrugged into his suit jacket, tucking his shirt in tighter and buttoning his jacket, looking all businessman perfect. I envied him a little, his ease at looking so deliciously gorgeous and perfectly pulled together just seconds after being enthralled in a frenzied, passionate moment, with me.

I, on the other hand, was a sight. And *not* a fan of being left in need. Which was new for me. Maybe that's what happened when you swore off men for a spell. You become a lustful, wanton hussy.

Reeling, I did my best to whip myself into shape as our driver gracefully climbed out of the car and came around to my door.

I took the driver's proffered hand and let him assist me to my feet.

Standing at the entrance of *Trump International Hotel and Tower Toronto*, the towering hotel with the room we'd be sharing tonight—or should I say…uh, the pleasure palace with the suite we'd be sinfully christening tonight—was both daunting and impressive. My head tipped back as I took in the entire glistening sight, seeming to touch the heavens.

The hum of anticipation fell over me as Adam swept up from behind and settled one of his large hands on my rear. My brows raised, and I gave him sideways glance, noting the look of innocence at contradiction with the sexy smirk on his lips. Nonetheless, he got the message, and his possessive hand slipped to the small of my back, instead.

Truth be told, I liked that possessive hand on me…

Chapter Three

I hung a few strides behind while Adam approached the glitzy reservation desk. A lanky young man with a chaos of red hair atop his head, the sides tucked in close, was eager to greet him. "Good evening, Sir. A reservation?" he asked in a surprisingly deep voice; which in no way matched his outward appearance.

"Yes. Under Blaire."

The reservation host's hazel eyes flicked to me, quickly swiping down my body.

"Mr. and *Mrs*. Blaire," Adam pressed (*slash* blatantly lied) with a severe tone and an accompanying warning glare, swinging the host's attention back his way. "Sneaking in a little second honeymoon with my beautiful bride." Adam winked one eye at him. "You know how it is."

Oh my.

Adam snatched the key card from the poor guy's stunned fingers.

Ooh! *We're really doing this*. I at once began questioning my decision to spend a sex filled night with Adam—isolated in a private hotel suite with a complete stranger, not a smart idea. A stranger. A hookup. *I'd let him pick me up on a flipping airplane, for crying out loud*! What the hell was I thinking?

In a panic, I started to back step; surely there'd be a cab out front to take me to another hotel? Maybe my originally intended hotel?

Adam returned with an uneasy expression marking his features.

I was curious to the expression. *Had he felt my doubt? My shameful remorse? My panic?*

Without hesitation, Adam slipped his hand in mine and pulled me to him, tucking me in close with my torso curled against the side of his.

Honestly, it was a little cuddlier and cozier than I'd expected, causing an uncomfortable awkwardness and increasing the heaviness in my chest.

Adam squeezed my hand. "We good, sweetheart?" And then he gave me that look; his heart melting smile and a panty dropping, sexy gaze with those mesmerizing bedroom eyes of his. *Swoon.* "Don't change your mind, Bethany, don't bail out on me," he pleaded. "Ecstasy awaits; a night of blissful ecstasy. A night to lose all self-control, let loose your inhibitions, and welcome intense passion and pleasure."

Ohhh...just like that I was back on board.

Adam ushered me to the elevators, needy urgency buzzing between us. *He still thinks I'm gonna chicken out*, I figured by the rush of his actions.

The elevator doors slid open and in the empty car we went.

Seeking a little distance from the buzzing need between us, I left Adam's side and moved to the far left side wall of the elevator. Adam settled against the right, facing me as I leaned my backside against the handrail.

Adam's hungry blue-green eyes smoothed over my body, caressing every skin tingling inch of me while they slowly drifted their way back to mine.

I bit my lower lip.

"You're a very beautiful woman, Bethany," he expressed in a soft, velvety smooth tone.

My thighs squeezed together, as if he'd whispered that soft, velvety smooth tone between them, stroking me with his breath.

It felt like several long hours before the elevator doors opened, the entire time thinking Adam was going to pounce. That look in his eyes... *Yikes!*

I pushed off the railing, ready to exit this hot box of lust and sexual tension, when five people—four men and one woman—crowded in.

My eyes flicked to the lit up floor numbers above the closing elevator door.

Damn. Five more floors to go.

I pushed back against the handrail, a big, husky cowboy suddenly in my space. "Well, hello there Darlin'. Aren't you a pretty little thing?"

I felt the heat of Adam's tension crackling in the air. From between the others, I caught sight of him, trapped in his spot against the right side wall, rigid. His eyes were narrowed and his brows pushed together, shooting daggers at the cowboy.

Oh my. *What is that look?*

The cowboy continued and my eyes snapped back to him, widening at his words. "—Can I interest you in a drink, Sweet Cheeks?"

I didn't know how, but Adam was instantly at my side, his arm possessively around my waist, clenching me into his side like I belonged there.

I felt breathless; like the wind had been sucked out of me.

"She's with me, big guy," Adam snarled. He kissed the top of my hair. "Married this one as soon as I could get her to say 'I do'."

What?!

Now *my* eyes narrowed, at Adam. (*Liar, liar pants on fire.*)

His hand slipped under the back of my blouse and dipped below the waistline of my skirt until he met bare flesh, settling in the dip at the small of my back.

And there it was, the surge of electricity from his touch; a direct *jolt* between my thighs, eliciting a pool of warm moisture in my center.

Adam must have known, because he let his hand glide a little farther down to the gentle slope of my rear, what I assumed was his pinky finger nestled between my butt cheeks. *Wow, the pure, bold hotness of this man...* I casually grabbed onto the handrail, my knees weakening beneath me, threatening to give way.

I bit back a moan; I was ready to climb him like a tree right then and there. His hand moved even farther down, somehow managing to squeeze both butt cheeks at once before it slipped away, sweeping possessively over my shoulders. He held his hand at the side of my neck, fingers kneading up into my hair from behind my ear. I moved into his hand—I might actually have moaned aloud—my eyes rolling back at the divine feeling, like a purring kitten or puppy reveling in her master's affectionate petting, enthralled.

Adam's hand gradually slipped down my neck, pressing at the base on my collarbone, locked on like a choker around my neck, completely possessive of me. An act that was meant to show the cowboy, as well as me, I supposed, that he possessed me.

Normally, that sort of action would have annoyed me, but to my great surprise, I liked it—being possessed by this man, still a stranger. *Way* more than I should have. He had me swooning. And my entire body singing.

"In fact," Adam went on, unaffected, "we're on a second honeymoon." He brushed the backs of his fingers over my warm, flushed cheek. "Aren't we, baby?" He met my eyes with a sparkle of mischief.

Baby?

When the hell are those elevator doors going to open?

The man was dangerous; disarmingly cute when he wanted to be, but dangerous!

Not to be deterred, Cowboy replied, "Up for sharing?"

Whoa! WTF?!

His dark eyes leered into mine before drifting to my lips for a prolonged period, and then sexually threatening the rest of my body before roaming back to my breasts.

Holy cow. *Why hadn't I worn a burlap sack today?*

"I don't mind watching, or being watched," cowboy creepily sneered.

Eww.

Adam lunged forward, chest and all, glaring up at the man with a look of menace. *He actually had to look up at the guy, the guy was so tall.*

In that moment, I was oblivious to the others in the elevator with us.

The cowboy tipped back from Adam. "Hey, no offense man, just wondering if you were into it. You know, a third partner."

Was this guy for real? The thought of him alone, made my skin crawl. No way in hell was he touching me! *Or* watching me, for that matter.

"I take complete offense, you dirty fuck," Adam growled in the man's face, "As does my lovely bride, I'm sure."

What the holy hell? Adam had the spark of the devil in him. Why would he say such a thing? Second honeymoon? Bride?

What the heck kind of game was he playing here?

The elevator doors at last opened. Adam right away yanked me out, his arm tight around my back and his hand firm on my hip, at a fast pace toward our room. I could barely keep up, my heels skittering along.

"What the hell was that?" I snapped at him. "Maybe I wanted that drink, or wanted to be with him."

Adam abruptly halted in his stride, halting me too, fingers digging into my hip and that menacing glare now turned on me.

Eek!

"Did you?" he spat.

I swallowed hard, my breath lodged in my chest.

"Did you?!" Adam repeated, startling me to jump with the abrasiveness in his tone.

My lashes fluttered up at him. "N—No," I stuttered softly.

"Okay, then." His grip on my hip softened, and he set back into shuffling us at a hurried pace toward our awaiting suite.

I dared challenging him. "But I could have said as much myself. I didn't need you to be my knight in shining armor, in a testosterone driven battle, having a pissing contest in a crowded elevator."

He chuckled. "That's what we men do."

"And what's with the wife and honeymoon farce?"

"That guy was a forward ass," Adam snarled. "I thought that would warn the dirty bastard off."

I rolled my eyes. *Says the man forward enough to give me, a complete stranger, a blissful thrill midair.* Though, that guy *was* an ass. "And at the reservation desk?" I raised a suspecting brow at him.

Adam grinned; that devilish one that stirred all kinds of sinful things on my insides. "That was just for fun. And to save your moral virtue."

Oh please? I think I surrendered the remaining remnants of my moral virtue on that plane.

And really, what did he care anyway?

We were finally at the door to our suite. Adam swiftly zipped the key card in and unlocked the door, quickly pushing it open and leading me on in as he held the door open with his body.

Unable to take the sparks of electricity and fire burning between us a second longer, the moment Adam kicked the door shut behind us, my skirt was up and Adam's arm was around the back of my waist, lifting me to the nearest wall as he roughly kissed me. The items I was carrying—my handbag and laptop case—dropped to the carpeted foyer floor as Adam worked feverishly on the button and zipper of his suit slacks while his demanding mouth consumed mine, claiming me with a passion so fierce I feared he'd devour me whole. Own me, mind, body and soul.

The faint sound of a zipper filled my ears, followed by the tear of a foil pack, and my legs instinctively wrapped around Adam's middle. His hand slapped to the wall, splayed out above my head, bracing us.

"I hope you're ready," he muttered in a rush, and then slammed into me. *I'd been ready since the illicit encounter mid-air.* We gasped against each other's mouth. Raw pleasure zinged through me. "Bethany," Adam gritted out as he held still inside me, absorbing the exquisite sensations stimulated upon the initial physical contact of our bodies joining, after what felt like a lifetime of waiting since that first jolt of desire, when we'd initially locked eyes on that plane.

Wow! This was already so much more than I'd ever felt before —the stimulation of him just being there…filling me…inside. My eyes fluttered closed. Flashes of blazing heat and need tingled and twitched inside me. And he'd yet to move!

My breaths came sharp and quick, my chest heaving, the fill of him—so full and so deep—was like no other.

We were a perfect fit.

Adam pulled out slowly, and then drove back in quickly, moving his hips at a hard, swift pace from there, hard thrust after wicked hard thrust, pleasure pulsing inside me.

My arms flew around his neck, my hands grasped at the back of his head tugging at his hair.

Holy hell.

It was fast, furious, frenzied, and hard. The connection with this man was unreal. We were like two flames combusting…two live wires sparking when they touched. My body was spiraling out of control in the blink of an eye. "Adam… Oh—"

Ahh, the man had skills; not only were his fingers magic…

"Not, yet," Adam groaned, sensing my imminent release.

Did he really think I could control it? I clenched around him. It was impossible to control.

"Ah, fuck, baby," he hissed.

I usually thought it was creepy when a man called me baby, but to hear it pass between Adam's luscious lips in that sexy, wanton, about-to-come-undone tone, it just sounded…*Hot*!

He rocked into me one more time, and let out an audible grunt. "Now!" he blew out.

Hallelujah!

I let the spiraling within unwind and allowed myself to lose all self-control, this once, to let everything else go and lose myself like I'd never done in the past, to feel every sensation, and succumb to the possibility of euphoric ecstasy and welcome all that Adam offered. Because if any man was ever going to elicit it—*sheer euphoric ecstasy*—it was Adam Blaire.

In that very moment, heaven shattered upon me and I came undone around him, my body trembling with an exquisite release, feeling Adam do the same. His hips kept moving, tiny pulses and thrusts, as his head fell forward, his face turned into the gentle curve of my neck and his lips parted, opened on my skin with panting breaths.

I nipped the top curl of his ear; it was just too close to resist. Adam's hips jerked in reaction, pleasurably nudging into me a little deeper and eliciting another flurry of trembling waves of aftershock.

Heavens, the connection with this man.

Adam's arm held firm around the back of my waist, a hand cupped at the nape of my neck and my legs still hooked around him, he pulled me from the wall and twisted toward the bedroom. Two strides in came a knock on the door. "Concierge," called a man from outside the door.

"Damn!" Adam cursed and growled, "Our bags." He scurried me into the bathroom—it was nearest—fumbling to tuck himself in and fasten his slacks as he set my feet to the cool stone flooring. "Wait there a second," he murmured on my cheek, giving me a quick kiss on his way out.

I stood there reeling, my legs somewhat wobbly from frenzied wall sex, missing the abrupt loss of our connection. I dared a peek at myself in the mirror. *Jesus*! I looked a disheveled mess. My hair a wild, chaotic tangle of dark curls. My shirt crumpled and hanging to one side. My skirt...well, let's just say I was exposed... And my cheeks—I bit my bottom lip with somewhat of a grin—perfectly pink and glowing. Fully ravished and devoured. *Taken*. That's how I looked. I'd never felt more amazing in my life. Were all one night stands-*slash*-casual hookups like this; this spectacular and mind-blowing? I couldn't help wondering. If so, I should have indulged a long time ago.

I was brought from my musings when I heard Adam's husky voice in the foyer, asking for champagne to be delivered. *That's definitely going to play havoc with my early morning meeting.* He ordered food, too; burgers, I thought I heard, and an entire chocolate cake. What's he thinking?

I righted my shirt on my shoulders and pulled down my skirt, raking my fingers through my tangled chaos of hair as I whirled around, marveling at the size of bathroom.

Good grief, it was bigger than my bedroom at home in my bungalow. Large clear glass enclosed shower taking up one entire end of the bathroom, to the right of where I was standing at the double sinks and sprawling mirror, and a Jacuzzi tub taking up the opposite far end. *Too bad there wouldn't be time to indulge and enjoy that tub. Or that shower, for that matter.*

The door blew open, Adam stalking nearer with purpose in his every step.

I swallowed, and my skin tingled in anticipation.

"We having a party?" I right away asked. No way were we eating a whole chocolate cake between us.

"Yeah, party for two," Adam quipped, his eyes glittering and intent in there gaze into mine as he reached me, and gathered me into his arms. "I figured we needed to refuel our energy," he murmured in explanation. "Especially you, you hardly ate on that plane,"

I put aside my surprise that he'd been watching me on the flight, paying close enough attention to my actions to pick up on the detail that I'd just nibbled at my meal. I hoped the detail of *why* I was unable to eat, had slid by without his notice; the mere fact that he'd had my insides all a jumble.

I reasoned, "It'll keep me up all night…eating that cake." *And chocolate at that*!

"That's what I'm hoping." Adam friskily wiggled his eyebrows at me, his features lit up with a naughty little grin. "I plan to make the most of my time with you, and I assure you that will take well into the morning hours."

Oh…the man was purely delicious.

"Come," he ordered, and then scooped me into his arms, groom-style, back en route to the bedroom. I felt the pitter-patter of my heart, a light and rapid flutter beneath the center of my chest. "We'll be making full use of that later," Adam threw out in reference to the tub and shower, once again reading my thought. He carried me through the foyer and past the wall of pleasure, winding through the living room to at last the master suite.

I hadn't noticed much about our hotel suite when we'd first entered—what with the frenzied need, and all—but now, as we swept through each room, I caught a quick peek. The suite was very elegant: pristine white walls and décor; glass and mirror tables and accents, balanced with black and silver furniture and drapery; surrounding floor to ceiling windows with an awe inspiring panoramic view of the Toronto city skyline and impressive Lake Ontario. The place reeked of wealth and elegance, down to the black and crystal chandeliers hanging in the living room and dining room. And the ambiance of a fire lit in the fireplace, was an especially nice touch.

A niggle of awareness flickered through me; nothing about this night appeared casual, it was all too perfect. Not to mention, how did Adam pull this off...? Was this suite always staged like this, romantic fire aglow? Or had Adam somehow arranged it? And was this his originally intended room, or had he made a change, with this night with me in mind? *Hmm*? Something told me I was never going to forget this night, or want to leave this room and this man.

The master suite was just as classy; spacious, with a like color and décor scheme as the rest we'd seen, and a similar lit fireplace with a pair of black velvet armchairs and a white fur rug angled before it. A surrounding wall of windows mesmerized, darkness falling beyond it and city lights twinkling as the glow of the fire flickered and danced on the ceiling and walls around us. *Wow*. The entire décor leant a look of modern elegance with an exquisite romantic ambiance. Though, my eyes were on the shimmery silvery-white comforter on the magnificent bed that Adam had at last found, and the beautiful black and crystal chandelier centered above it.

Truthfully, the only thing absent from completing the perfectly romantic scene, were the velvety rose petals loosely scattered about the room and bed. Thank goodness.

Adam gently laid me on the bed, his body quickly hovering over me. "Now that that's out of the way..." I got the impression he was referring to the initial frenzied, passionate comingling against the foyer wall, and not the interruption by the concierge. "I need to see you," he rasped, eyes flashing dark. "Then I need to taste you, slow and sweet."

Good God, that was *hot*. Another shudder ripped through my body in response, stirring up yet another burst of aftershocks.

Oh, the man was the gift that just kept giving.

His face over mine, just a mere inch away, I could feel the swiftness of Adam's breath dizzying my head. A hand at my hip smoothed up my torso, cupping my breast while warm lips touched mine, soft and sweet, a zipper and the hardness beneath firm on me, grinding against the slow spasming of aftershocks, vowing all kinds of promises—promises, I prayed would be kept.

I clung onto his biceps.

With smooth dexterity Adam's fingertips undid each button of my blouse and whispered it open, revealing skin baring lavender lace, leaving nothing to his imagination.

A deep groan escaped Adam's chest, fingertips lightly tracing over each breast. He popped the front hook, exposing me completely. A sudden rush of cool air brought my breasts to attention as a delightful chill passed over my entire body. I felt a slight whimper hum between my lips. I was lost.

Adam's body suddenly left mine and he was on his knees, poised between my feet. "Put your feet on the bed, legs spread," he demanded, startling me from my blissful reverie, the feeling of his touch and what he was doing to me.

"Pardon?"

"Now!" he hissed at me.

For reasons other than I could, nor wanted to, understand, I wholeheartedly wanted to please Adam; the harsh command of his voice did unspeakable things to me. Naughty, things.

My legs snapped up, knees bent, feet flat on the mattress and my heart pounding in my chest, literally heaving in anticipation.

"Beautiful," Adam blew out in a breath, his shimmering eyes taking me all in.

He smirked, his tongue darting out and licking his lips. *Apparently he liked what he was seeing*. And then something magical happened; my feet spread farther apart, fully opening up for Adam, all shyness and self-consciousness falling away—a move on my part I was stunned by.

Adam's eyes locked on mine. He crawled toward me, a wicked, feral look in his oceany eyes as he dipped his head between my parted thighs. That animalistic look... I *loved* being his prey.

The first long, slow stroke with his tongue, my body shuddered and my hands tightly clenched the sheets on either side of me. *What the hell?*

I felt the pulse of Adam's breath beat against my moist heat and knew he was chuckling. He showed no mercy, my reaction only encouraging him to plunge his tongue in, deeper and deeper.

Okay... so his fingers weren't the only thing magic...

That tongue... Oohhh...he had amazing skills with that

tongue. He'd clearly done this a time or two. I found myself thankful for the women before me to which he'd practiced and perfected his heavenly skills. And that thought swiftly vanished, wiped away when I felt Adam's fingers move inside. Today's shenanigans on the plane flooded into thought, that sinful first touch, and my hips bucked up. Adam clamped down on my delicate flesh, fingers thrusting fast, and I was once more lost, stars shimmering and fireworks exploding behind my eyelids as I completely shattered beneath this man.

I thought he'd stop then, after bringing me to such astounding completion, but instead a third finger entered, thrusting and curling and circling with the other two, reaching to all the special sweet spaces within while his tongue continued to show love too, my body trembling hard around him. Relentless, he was— bringing on two more earth-shattering releases.

Holy mother of…

At last, he was climbing up me, moving up to join in. I was spent; in such a way that was completely heavenly, and mind muddling. Adam's lips pressed to mine with a kiss before I'd even registered what he was doing; that he was sharing. "Taste what I did to you," he murmured, "taste what I taste." *I swear*, I felt another one coming on, building and bundling the nerves and muscles of pleasure and desire in all my secret spots. How was that even possible? I was bone weary already.

"You're the devil, Mr. Blaire."

Adam faintly laughed, flashing me a wicked smirk, "Only with you." And then he entered me in one long, slow, excruciating drive. "I'll be whatever you want me to be, angel; drag you into a sinful heaven with me."

Ohhh…a sinful heaven indeed.

I put myself in the hands of the Pleasure Master. The maestro to my instrument, exploring all the wondrous, never before explored capabilities of my body, and making it sing with pleasure.

Coupling with Adam was perfection.

Just as before, the fill of him, resting there, taking it all in, was something to behold. Though this time was somehow more intimate, having Adam lying over me instead of taking me hard and quick against the wall, those sea blue bedroom eyes piercing into my own as he remained still.

A niggle of fear squirmed and reared at the back of my muddled mind, and I just as quickly pushed it away, into the muddled mass of my pleasure occupied brain. *Denial*, it's a good thing; *think like a man, Beth, not a feely girl, that's where you get into trouble. Sex without strings, a mere hookup to feel good and move on.* I can do this!

I ran my hands along Adam's lower stomach, hard muscle after hard ridge of muscle, my happy fingers dancing impishly up to his chest—*more hard, glorious muscle*—until my fingers slowed and spread out, my palms memorizing every detail of this gorgeous hunk of man on their slow journey. Adam started to move and my legs intuitively melded around the curve of his backside, taking him in deeper. It was all happening in slow motion, lost as I was in those eyes and submerged in every pleasurable feeling Adam elicited. Before I knew it my hands had fascinated their way over his throat, my thumbs doing most of the enthralled exploring and memorizing as they drew to his lips. *Oh, those lips.* My eyes watched, mesmerized, as my fingertips sensuously sketched and outlined. I couldn't help myself, I pressed one wicked finger past those luscious, full, pleasure evoking lips, slipping it along his masterful tongue and then in and out, in my own little hypnotized world.

"Ahh…what are you doing to me?" Adam groaned around my finger, hard and feverishly sucking it into his mouth and then releasing it as his hips ground against me. "Screw slow!" He flipped me to my hands and knees, a hand hard pressed on my lower stomach, slamming into me from behind as the room settled its spin. *Whoa.* He'd moved so fast I hadn't felt it happen and wasn't sure if he'd even left me during the move; broken our intimate contact during the shift. He held my hips tipped up, a hand gripped firm on each hip while I did my part to meet his every thrust and rock of his hips.

Bless the man. He tried to take it slow as promised—a slow and sweet trip to heaven—but ultimately gave in to the wild desire between us. It was pretty hard to deny. Though, Adam *had* kept his vow to drag me in to a *sinful heaven* with him, the wicked devil that he was—which was a zillion times better, I thought; all that eye contact and dreamy touchy feely, was messing with my head in a big way. And we were both sated—me, like I'd never been—and exhausted; our desire fully gratified. *At least momentarily.*

The weight of Adam's body fell onto my back, his lips on the sensitive curve of my neck and shoulder, sucking to the point where pleasure and pain mingled.

"You're going to leave a mark," I murmured.

"Yes, I am," he said matter-of-factly, his mouth clamping down even harder and drawing on my skin with purpose.

My insides smiled. *Could the man be any more delicious?*

I was surprisingly okay with being claimed with the mark of Adam's passion; at least for the sake of living in the moment and letting it all go, to open myself up to the experience of a one night hookup.

So I told myself.

I collapsed to the bed on my stomach, taking Adam with me and nearly crushing myself with the heft of his body—but in a good way. His body consumed mine, surrounding me with manly hard muscle and sex sweaty skin, lending a sense of comfort and safety. If only for the time being.

"Watching you breaking right before my eyes, completely coming apart..." Adam murmured hot in my ear, "I could watch it a million times over. There's nothing like it." He rolled from my back to his own and then slid me on top of him, his strong hands clenched on my ass. "Then to feel you watching me, rapt... Jesus, Bethany, sweetheart. That was the sexist thing I've ever... Damn." His lips found mine, lingering warmth gliding along my lips, his tongue indulging in a deep, languorous caress with mine that lit my insides on fire and brought tingles to my skin, teasing desire anew. Mercy!

Adam's lips slipped from mine, soft kisses fluttering delightfully across my cheeks, my jaw, my chin, my throat, and my neck while wicked hands had their way with my backside.

Adam whispered between ardent kisses on my neck, "I have a feeling our food's arrived."

"What?!" My head snapped up. "While we were—"

He flashed me a haughty grin, "Yes. I instructed the concierge to enter and leave us undisturbed."

"Oh God." Sheesh, he must have heard; I was screaming and moaning loud enough to peel the elegant paint from the suite walls, and curl a few toes nearby.

"I think it's gonna have to wait a bit longer—"

Ooh. And we were at it again. An ardent kiss planted roughly on my lips…

Chapter Four

Lying leisurely fireside, our bellies fully sated from our delicious burgers and fries, Adam refilled my glass with champagne and placed the bottle back in the ice bucket behind him.

Earlier, Adam had insisted on grabbing two pillows and taking our shenanigans to the floor in front of the fireplace, to eat our dinner picnic-style. (*Adam, sweet man, was a bit of a romantic... who would have guessed?*)

He'd also insisted on wrapping my bare body in the big ole luxury comforter from the bed and carrying me to the lush, white fur rug before the fire. *He* was gloriously—thank God—naked! All during dinner. Talk about distracting. I scarfed my burger down in record time, aware of his body's readiness to move on to our naughty doings—the purpose of the night; immoral shenanigans-*slash*-sexcapades. I nearly choked on my food in my eagerness. Although, I wondered how that was possible, that Adam lacked the need for rebound time?

"You ever done this before?" Adam surprised me by asking.

"What? Have wild, crazy, blissfully naughty sex with a complete stranger? A one night stand? A hookup?" Questioning brows rose high above my wide eyes. "No! Never!" I didn't need to ask Adam the same question; that answer was abundantly clear.

"Not even a fumbling quickie, maybe during your college years?" he pressed.

"Nope."

"Why me, then?"

Jeez. Because you're absofreakinlutely gorgeous and have a rockin' hard body and a sexy megawatt smile, that does all kinds of naughty things to me—causing me to want to return the naughty favor. But clearly I couldn't tell him that. So I shrugged my shoulders and took a quick sip of my champagne. *Yummy and bubbly.* Adam took a longer sip, waiting me out.

I inhaled a big breath and let it out, eyeing him propped casually on his side at my feet, massaging an instep with his thumb. "It was something Lizzy said when she was dropping me off at the airport for my flight."

"Oh?"

"Something along the line of me needing to loosen up, and find my mojo." Ugh! That made me sound so pathetic. "I think her exact words were… 'A hot man is exactly what you need to shake it up and get yourself out of this slump you're in.' I wasn't very receptive to her advice," I admitted. "The last thing she said to me was, 'One night stand, baby!' giggling as I shut the car door on her." It still irked me now, that Lizzy'd been so damn pushy about it. Adam bit back a grin, pursing his lips mercilessly. "Basically, she gave me a swift kick in the ass, though unwanted as it was. I'd sworn off men."

Adam kissed the tip of my big toe, the backs of his fingers sweeping up the lower portion of my leg, like a force on fire.

"And then there you were, bringing all your sexy to the seat next to me," I said. "And I didn't take you for a stalker, serial killer or rapist."

A lopsided grin swept menacingly across Adam's features. "Oh, I could stalk you." He crawled me like a wild animal, and I giggled like a teenage schoolgirl.

"You're a gorgeous woman, Bethany, and surely the sexiest thing I've ever seen," he growled.

Oh my. *Me?* I worked one side of my bottom lip between my teeth.

He was right at me, lips hovering over my own. *Hot, hot, hot!* "And the unbelievable fact that you seem to not even know it, is a massive turn on and is doing wicked, crazy things to me." As if to accentuate his words, Adam ground the evidence against my thigh.

My gut clenched. As well as my girly bits. In a soft, tentative breath, I whispered, "You're not uneasy on the eyes, either, Mr. Blaire."

"Is that so?" A reverent kiss touched my lips, rapidly picking up heat.

I was sprawled out on that fur rug on the floor before I knew it—in a very unladylike way— the comforter pulled open, baring me to him. My skin goose pimpled from the sudden shock of cool air, at contrast to the fire burning within as Adam's eyes stole a slow, languorous gaze over the length of my body.

His lips came crashing down on mine once more, demanding and crushing, his thumb rubbing the distended peak of my nipple and the hard heat between his hips pressing into me, teasing. I moaned into Adam's mouth, sliding my tongue along his, loving what he was doing to me, how absolutely crazy he was making me.

My fingernails grazed down the length of his sides, and my hands clamped onto his butt cheeks, pushing him firmer against me.

Adam slipped from on top of me to lie beside me, his head on my breast, cozied up into my side as his tongue carried on the assault on my nipple. I curled my fingers in his hair, letting the tendrils of thick, dark hair slide between my fingers, taking a moment to catch my breath and slow my wild heart rate.

Adam's large hand gently cupped between my parted legs, one finger tenderly nestled in between, finding home.

A mini jolt of electricity sparked through me, stirring my arousal and pulling at my core.

Dear Lord, could I really be ready for more?

I felt a subtle flood of moisture beneath Adam's hand, and had my answer. YES!

Adam looked up at me; I mean *really* looked at me—he too felt moisture—his eyes smoldering and lust filled, drowning me in their heat. He shifted his body and moved up mine, his lips on the curl of my ear and his finger pushing in a little deeper. "I'm going to make damn sure you remember me with every step you take tomorrow; possibly clear into next week."

Oh my. YES! YES! YES! PLEASE! Screamed out in my head.

"I'm ready for my dessert… " Adam growled, "And by dessert …I mean *you*."

My heart pounded, thumping in my ears, another shot of liquid heat pooling down deep in my belly.

My hips bucked against his hand. "Jesus—" I hissed, feeling a sweet clenching below.

"I've already told you," Adam murmured low and husky, "Jesus, has nothing to do with it, sweetheart." His breath blew warm against my neck, swirling in an intoxicating whirl of temptation over my skin and tantalizing my senses. *Hell, the man smelled good. Who has breath that devastating and yummy?* And the virile, masculine scent of him lingering all around me, on the comforter, in the air and on our skin, only intensified that intoxication. I breathed in deeply: spicy, manly, sex, and all yumminess.

"Arms on top of the pillow, sexy," Adam's sudden demand struck my ear, snapping me from my fascination with his scent.

I looked at him a little curious, but did exactly what he'd asked, every nerve and cell of my being now intrigued and alerted to him. My arms laid against the pillow, stretched out at either side of my head, waiting, my fingers wiggling and twitching in anticipation above my head.

Adam leisurely smoothed his hand along my skin—fingers spread out with light pressure, really feeling, touching to my very soul—from my armpit up the inside of my arm, sashaying across the palm of my hand to my fingers, tenderly tickling up and down each digit, tip to palm and lacing between, in and out, and then moving back down the inside of my arm, down the softness of my side and swishing briefly across my belly, searing a white-hot trail of fire gliding over my hip to my thigh as his lips and tongue caressed my breast, teeth grazing. A slow, agonizing dance alerting my nipples to his intensions and assuring receptiveness before slithering down and nestling between my legs. He spread them farther apart. "Don't move, sweetheart. Just lie there, let me... This is all me, pleasuring you."

Oh, wow.

Didn't he already do that?

Thrice?

And then thrice more?

But I relented, and once again put myself in the magically skilled hands of the Pleasure Master.

Bless him. Adam was a generous lover; the most generous lover I'd ever been with. That's already more "O"s in one night than in the entire duration of my last relationship. *Pretty much the sum of* all *my relationships.*

Why *had* I wasted my time then?

Adam suddenly tipped his glass of champagne up over my chest, pouring a steady stream that ran down the valley between my breasts and pooled in the well of my bellybutton. My stomach did an inward *jerk* at the initial sensation of the chilled liquid hitting the heat of my skin, but I held the champagne there, moving not another muscle while Adam kept on with his play. He flashed that wicked, mischievous grin, droplets of champagne hitting one nipple and then the other, both stiffening at the shock, my nether regions clenching and throbbing in reaction. "Gah!" Adam's teeth clamped onto one distended bud, administering a kind of blissful torture while his finger and thumb assaulted the other. My body was squirming on the inside, already desperately wanting to writhe and to arch up in response, but I was trapped, unable to move or I'd spill the bubbly liquid in my bellybutton before Adam got to it. I didn't want to miss that!

Mmm, and there he was, both hands on my breasts, and his mouth and tongue lapping up the tasty trail from the valley between to the teensy pool at my belly. The feel of that mouth and tongue on my skin, I swear, in that moment, was the best feeling I'd ever felt.

My body was on *fire*, burning at the slow torture, wild with desire. Adam's tongue swirled along my skin, sure to rid all remnants of champagne, at last dipping into my button and sucking thoroughly, with conscientious effort.

Holy Hell, this man was fun!

He moved a little lower, his tongue and lips still swirling and nipping and kissing; my belly, to my hips, and to the sweet valley below, pausing on the uppermost inside part of my thigh, the delicate hollow of soft, smooth skin at the junction of my thigh and center—one of the softest, most smoothest part of skin on a woman, able to breathe in her essence. *Mmm*, Adam hummed, followed by a low growl deep in his chest, his lips locking down and loving hard, leaving me a reminder of this moment with him, of our time together.

It was incredibly erotic, the sensations elicited from Adam sucking there, so close, the vibration, pulsing and contracting deep inside... He was driving my wild!

And then the remainder of champagne left his glass, poured over the essence at my center and trickling between; an electrifying jolt snapped at my core and bolted through my veins. *That did it*, my hips left the fur rug and pushed against Adam's mouth, needing him closer. He kept my legs spread apart and swiftly set after it: tongue, mouth, sucking, and licking...his breath—*Sweet Jesus!*—blowing hot on my wetness. It hit me quick; my arms stretched out further above my head and my hands grabbed onto the short chair legs, bracing myself for the tumbling torrent I knew was coming and begging in a panted breath for Adam to join me, "I want you, Adam, please," needing our bodies connecting like a man and women do, the age old dance for centuries shared, to feel him reach in and touch my insides, not wanting to tumble over alone; I *so* wanted to take him with me.

Adam bit gently, sucked hard, and with the glow of candlelight and fire flickering and crackling he sent me blissfully tumbling and violently crashing, my trembling body writhing. Guttural screams filled my ears; to my surprise, *my own*. "Fucking hell, Adam!" My quivering legs clamped onto his upper back, Adam's fingers pushing in, at last joining the party. Wave after wave, this time harder than anything I'd ever felt; one torrent following another as Adam relentlessly kept on, softening his touch but his mouth never leaving contact with my hypersensitive sweet pearl. Caress after caress, and thrust after thrust of his fingers, one passionate release hit after the other, tumultuous waves slapping against the fine, white sandy ocean shore until I crumbled, and my body went limp—subtle pulsing and delicate aftershocks still rolling and humming inside. *Good God.* "Adam," I breathed, his tongue taking one more long, gentle swipe through his reward, the sweetness released from his labors. My head lay heavy against the pillow, the effort to lift it far too great. *Holy hell, holy hell, holy hell!* That was euphoric.

"I think you liked that," Adam chuckled.

I'd have laughed with him if I had the strength left in me. Instead, a sound something equivalent to a whimper and hum mix escaped between my lips.

He kissed my bellybutton tenderly and laid the side of his face on my stomach, his arms holding me tight at my hips and sides.

My arms fell from the pillow above my head, one hand unconsciously caressing Adam's hair, in a purely natural gesture, the other limp at my side, at rest on Adam's arm.

He found my hand and drew it closer to him, kissing the tip of each of my fingers. When he reached my pinky, he took it into his mouth with a gentle suck and swirl of his tongue.

"No—" I weakly moaned in protest, my overly, *overly* sensitized bits clenching and pulsing in reaction.

Adam held my hand against his cheek, his face sandwiched between my stomach and palm.

"I think you're trying to kill me, Mr. Blaire." I sighed. "Either that, or I've blissfully died and gone to heaven." *I'm going with heaven.*

"I told you; all about *me*, pleasuring *you*." He brushed a light kiss to the inside of my wrist, the tip of his nose gliding along the soft, delicate skin, taking in the scent before he held my palm back to his cheek. "Though, that must be a record; I'm sure of it. The way you respond as you do... the little noises that you make ...the moans and whimpers, wiggling and squirming... your oh sweet scent... Damn, I blame it on intoxication, the headiness of it all. It suddenly became a personal challenge to make you moan, whimper and wiggle; to see how many times I could make you scream my name; how long I could keep you there, teetering on the edge of ecstasy, before falling hard into euphoria; to see how many times I could bring you to consecutive… How many would be possible…" he stammered and trailed off, momentarily pausing. "I hadn't imagined you were such a high achiever, sweetheart."

I had no words. I mean, really, it wasn't like I could be *upset* with the outcome of his personal challenge. I was most definitely the one who benefited…*and* benefited and benefited. *I didn't even know my body was capable of such wondrous pleasure; a secret I am* thrilled *to have revealed.*

I briefly wondered if it was just in response to Adam, the electricity and pull between us, or if it'd been possible all along, with others, waiting to be drawn out?

Adam lifted his head from my stomach. With my eyes still closed, I felt him creep up me a bit, placing a gentle kiss to my lips. "You're amazing…the way you give yourself over to me," he whispered softly. "Thank you for surrendering to my control." Leaning close for another kiss, he cupped my face with both hands, the tip of his tongue parting my lips with a gentle tease against my own, causing a flurry of flutter in my belly. "Let's get you to bed, sweetheart."

His body left mine, to my surprise leaving me with a feeling of loss momentarily. Until I was thoroughly wrapped with the luxurious comforter and then surrounded in the comforting embrace of Adam's arms, being carried off to the bed.

Adam gently laid me on the bed sheets, the backs of his fingers brushing across my cheek in a languorous stroke, before he reverently kissed my forehead. "Rest a moment, baby."

He didn't need to tell me twice. I couldn't move if I wanted to. *Mercy, I was weary; he'd really taken it out of me.* My lower extremities were so limp I wasn't even sure if they were still attached to the rest of my body anymore. Adam wasn't kidding about wanting me to remember him with each step tomorrow— hell, I wasn't sure I'd be able to take a step at all, let alone *walk*, period!

Chapter Five

I stirred thirty minutes later, my eyes flittering open to Adam propped up beside me against the headboard, the chocolate cake in his lap—his *naked* lap! "Hungry?" he asked with a sweet smile.

I was suddenly ravenous. And not just for cake. "Yes," I whispered, my throat dry and fatigued. *Oh…oh God, I was screaming… Wow. Who knew I was a screamer?*

Certainly not me!

"Down, tiger," Adam said beside me, looking altogether too amused. "Cake, first."

Huh? *Wait—what?* How'd he know that? That I was craving more than cake? "I know, that's—"

"I see that glazed, heated look in those beautiful, pale blue eyes."

Pssh. "You wish, Mr. Blaire." I sat upright, keeping myself covered in the comforter. *Why I suddenly felt shy, was beyond me. The man had seen more of me than I had myself.*

"Cold?" he questioned, a sly smile on his features and a twinkle in his eyes when I turned my body to face him.

"No." I blinked up at him.

"Good. Then let's lose this." He tugged at the comforter,

pulling it away from my body and flipping it back behind me, sending the large pile of down tumbling mostly to the floor, off the side of the bed. A shiver sprinted over my skin from the sudden shock of air. Or, maybe it was just Adam's blazing gaze honed in on my nipples that were dutifully saluting him. "Much better," he said, tipping to me with a quick kiss.

I wasn't so sure about that.

"I think you should sit with your legs crossed; you know, Indian style."

I cocked a brow at him. *Hmph*! Pervert. "I will if you will." I grabbed the serving tray with the cake on it from his lap and set it on the mattress between us.

Adam shot me a sexy, mischievous smile, as if to say, "Okay, I'll play your game; I'm not shy." He shifted his body from the headboard to face me straight on, and tucked those long, strong, muscular, tanned legs into a crossed position—he looked like a delicious pretzel, with those slabs of muscle all twisted and knotted up—leaving his glorious manhood, marvelously *untucked*.

All the breath left my lungs.

There was that *distraction* again, just as with dinner. Adam may be able to handle this game just fine, but I now realized I may not. I already ached for him.

Adam gestured with his brows and a slight nod of his head, prodding me to follow suit; he'd met my challenge!

Seriously, what was I thinking? This was so out of character for me. I'd never been sexually bold. Ever! Why now? What was it about this man that made me want to do everything he asked?

With my still somewhat noodley legs extended in front of me, I uncrossed my ankles and brought my legs in, finagling them into a crossed sitting position; one ankle under each thigh, Indian style, like a child sitting in a circle for playtime—*Naughty* playtime! In my case.

"Ahh. Perfect way to eat sweet, decant chocolate cake... With an even sweeter view."

"You're a naughty man, Mr. Blaire."

"Right back at ya, sweets. And you love it, you know it." He tapped a finger on the tip of my nose, then on my bottom lip, his body angling closer for his lips to shadow his finger.

I pulled back, successfully dodging his impending kiss. "Down, *tiger*," I quipped, repeating his earlier words to me. "I see that glazed, heated look in those beautiful, blue-green bedroom eyes. Cake, first!"

Adam threw his head back with laughter. "Touché." Then he leaned that big body to me and stole his kiss anyway. "Let's eat cake, and get to know each other a little better, then."

"I think I know all I need to know about you, Mr. Blaire." I had hoped to keep a little distance for a bit, to avoid things getting too cozy; to keep the sex on the surface and elude intimacy. I needed to be able to walk away; knowing little about him would help that. No emotions, just sex! Adam wasn't making that easy though.

"Just the same, humor me, please."

No…he wasn't making it easy, *at all*.

Adam picked up the silver serving knife sitting on the tray alongside the cake—beside two silver lined cream plates, fancy silver forks, and elegant cream and silver swirled linen napkins—and used it to cut into the cake. The first cut into those layers of moist, gooey chocolate, my stomach growled. That cake had to be six inches tall, at least. My stomach growled again, this time even louder.

Adam snickered, and I rubbed my hand over my belly, hoping it'd help squelch, or at least somehow muffle, the sound.

Flipping the serving knife upright, Adam served a rather large slice of cake onto one of the plates, using the side of one of the forks to section off a smaller piece.

With his fingers and thumb on either side of the smaller piece he'd just cut, Adam hand fed me, urging me to part my lips so he could slide it between. The second that cake passed my lips, bittersweet chocolate burst across my tongue and exploded tastiness in my mouth. *Mmm*, I groaned in delight, my eyelids closing and my eyes rolling back in my head. There was something ceremonial about it, and altogether too *hot*! It was a whole other kind of ecstasy.

Adam popped the remainder into his own mouth, licking the deliciousness from his fingers. *Holy hell*, my knees snapped up, pressing together to crush the sudden spasm.

Adam chuckled, "I think you need another."

Of course, he did.

"And not fair—" He swatted the outer side of my thigh, "Back in position!"

Sheesh! *Bossy pants*. My knees separated and relaxed back down into their previous crossed position in front of me, affording Adam *his view*.

Another bite of cake came my way, Adam's eyes gleaming as he watched it enter my mouth, my tongue darting out to lick my lips. *Darn, if it wasn't the best cake ever*. I reached for a piece for Adam, thinking I'd give him a turn, but he swatted at my hand, "I'm in charge."

I narrowed my gaze at him, but held there waiting for his next move.

His fingers toyed with another piece of cake, taking a large chunk of shaved chocolate from the edge and bringing it to my mouth. He teasingly traced it across my bottom lip before he slid it in, along with the tip of his finger, letting it linger idly before slipping it back out.

"So tell me, sweetheart, how was it, really, that you knew I'd arrived to the airport in a limousine? Since I didn't believe for one second that it was a *lucky guess*, or that I looked *the type*."

Damn.

I finished chewing, pondering the words to explain.

I was hesitant, but finally gave it up and confessed. "I mentioned the swift kick in the butt my friend Lizzy had given me when she was dropping me off at the airport, and her remark that a hot man was exactly what I needed to shake it up and get myself out of the so-called slump she felt I was in; pushing me toward a one night stand…" God, I so didn't want to tell him this. "Well, *you*, were actually the exact man she had referred to." I turned my gaze to my fidgeting fingers, avoiding those eyes boring into me. "We were parked behind your limousine and saw you get out of the car, then watched you standing there momentarily, buttoning your perfectly tailored suit jacket while you waited for your driver to retrieve your bag." *There*, I said it. I risked a glance back up at Adam, swinging my eyes to his.

"I see," Adam said, his voice impassive as he spoke, as well as his expression. It was nerve-wracking. He couldn't really be up-set about what I'd shared? Could he? I wondered. "So you were dishonest with me, when I'd asked about it."

Oh, hell. "No. I wasn't dishonest. I just left a few details out..." That sounded even more pathetic than my earlier explanation, when he'd first asked. "—Details that I didn't find pertinent for you to know."

"And, now?"

"Are you asking me for the details?"

"Yes." A piece of cake was calmly passed between his lips, giving me a chance to confess the whole conversation with Lizzy, to share the *details* I'd left out the first time around. *Lord*. Really, I didn't see what the big deal was all about.

Except for my own embarrassment and humiliation, of course.

"Lizzy saw you first, just before I was about to get out of her family van. She was giving me *her* version of a pep talk, telling me to 'Rock those Toronto executives with our mad designs and killer ad plan, and show 'em how us kickass California girls' do it!'" That brought a slight curl to Adam's lips. "Then she added, 'And while you're at it...maybe you can rock one of those, too, *him*, and get yourself out of this slump you're in.' Feeling insulted that Lizzy'd implied that I'd lost my mojo and needed to loosen up, I followed her gaze out the front windshield, seeing you for the first time as she said... 'That type of man is exactly what you need to shake it up.' That's when she threw out the 'One night stand, baby!' remark, giggling her ass off."

I left out the part about thinking he was drool worthy HOT! That I thought he was complete perfection. And that I'd referred to him as 'A wealthy, pompous control freak businessman who disarmingly flits from one shattered female heart to the next...' That I'd assumed he wouldn't want a girl like me. Or, more importantly, that my heart had skipped and paused a beat... But I did say, "I was waiting for the lovely long legs of a beautiful woman to follow you out of the opened car door."

Adam slid right past that last remark. "So you'd seen me before I sat next to you on the plane," he said, casually securing another small piece of cake and resuming his quest to hand feed me. *Who was I to argue?* I took his finger in my mouth, whirling and twisting my tongue over and along it, shooting for a little seductive play. *A distraction.* Making an obscene show of licking the remains from his finger. Adam's eyelids partially closed, and a low groan escaped his chest, but he held his cool, seeming unflappable, not a bit deterred from his line of inquiry. "And you'd made your assumptions about me, based on *first sight*; not upon the first sight of me at your side on the plane, but the unloading zone, from some thirty feet away?"

I subtly nodded my head, feeling a little guilty; which made absolutely no sense at all.

"Seems to me, like our paths were destined to cross. Some kind of Divine Intervention," Adam murmured with a bit of a swagger. "The irony that your friend would single me out, of you seeing me, and the likelihood among thousands of travelers and a multitude of flights, that I was led to the seat beside you...? If that doesn't sound like fate—" His fingers left my lips and he lunged at me with a kiss, "I'd say you are out of the slump," licking the remnants of chocolate from my lips. *Scrumptious.* "If you were really even in one...I find it hard to believe."

"Oh," I moaned, "you can believe it."

"And I'm *lovin'* your *mojo*," he growled. "Tell your friend to back off; no loosening up needed." He fed me another bite, then himself, lunging on me again, this time tracing his tongue over my lips, playfully biting my bottom lip. "What'd you think on first sight?" he friskily whispered on my lip.

Oh, *soo* not going there. "Your turn, Mr. Blaire," I returned in a panted breath, dodging an answer to the question he'd just asked. "I shared details, now it's your turn."

Adam twisted to the bedside table and snatched up our glasses of champagne, twisting back and handing one off to me. He lifted his glass up for a toast. "To the beauty of first sight," he said in a buttery smooth voice.

I met my champagne glass to Adam's with a clink, echoing his words, "To the beauty of first sight." *And meddlesome, pushy best friends*, I thought to myself. We each took a sip from our glass, indulging in a moment of silence while we enjoyed our champagne.

Not bothering with the serving knife to cut into the cake for another slice, Adam used his fingers to scoop out my next bite.

"What details can I shed light on for you, sweetheart." He pushed the gooey blob of cake into my mouth, licking the remains from his fingers and thumb. I felt a pang of jealousy, certain I would have preferred licking those fingers and that thumb of the chocolaty remains, instead of eating the piece he'd fed me. "As I've already told you, I'm an open book."

Yeah, well... "What's a Beverly Hills divorce attorney, doing in Toronto?" I'd wondered that since he'd first mentioned his profession. "And how long... I mean, are you checking out in the morning?"

I mean, what are the chances we'd be on the same return flight?

"'*Best*' divorce attorney in Beverly Hills," Adam corrected me, singing his own praise with pride. But I guess it's the title he earned with skill and hard work; he *should* be proud of it. *Damn* proud!

"Yes, my mistake, Mr. Blaire. What is the *best* divorce attorney in Beverly Hills, doing in Toronto? Assuming you are here on business."

Adam's face lit with a smile, and he reached to my cheek and swept my hair back, tucking it behind my ear. "I'm in Toronto to help a friend out," he explained, seeming far away as his finger traced the curl of my ear. "And I'm staying through the weekend. The first two nights here, in this hotel suite. And then my friend has asked that I stay my last night with her, at her home."

Oh.

"She has made plans," Adam continued, his smile growing bigger, "but is keeping them a surprise until I see her."

This shouldn't have bothered me... Not in the least. But it did. *What the hell?*

"An old girlfriend?" I shot for nonchalance in my tone, but was unsure if that's how it came out. Because inside, I was reeling a bit at the shrieking reality in my head, '*Holy shit! He's already hooking up with someone else, has another woman actually lined up, that's how little I mean to him. How casual this is.*

"No." Adam's finger slid behind my ear, sashaying down the side of my neck, inducing a delicious shiver to course down my spine and spread across my shoulders.

"*Present*, girlfriend, then?" I asked somewhat hesitantly. I maybe should have asked the girlfriend question *before* I hussied it up with the man and engaged in mind-blowing sweaty sex with him.

"No," Adam replied. He seemed a teeny bit annoyed with my asking. "I mentioned that to you already, on the plane, when you asked if I was married."

Oops. That's right. *Jeez.* How had I forgotten that conversation?

Oh, yeah; because he'd just pleasured me on a crowded plane, bringing about a blissful haze!

"Are you *jealous*, baby?" A haughty grin snapped up and sparked across Adam's features, pleased.

Ha! "No. Makes no difference to me whom you spend your time with, or how, Mr. Blaire."

"Right." Adam snickered. "You're not a very good liar." He paused for a bite of cake, looking far too amused and delighted. "My friend, Sicily, is not an ex-girlfriend, but an old college roommate."

I fought the urge to roll my eyes. Of course he had roomed with a female. The man was entirely too charming, and had more animal magnetism than should be legally allowed.

"We lived together for four years, before we parted ways: she for med school, and I for law school," he explained, continuing on. "We've always kept in contact, with occasional visits, and phone calls varying from weekly to daily, depending on time and need."

I had to ask. "And you never, not even once, hooked up?"

"Never. Not even once." He blinked. "But one of our other roommates, Marcus, well, that is another story."

Ah. Adam hadn't lived with Sicily alone. That made better sense. "How many of you roomed together?"

"Three of us guys, and Sicily. It was a fairly good size house. Our other roommate, Jasper, the place belonged to his grand-parents, and they'd rented it to us for a steal." Adam's eyes casu-ally slid from mine as he ventured a peek at my bare chest, his eyes narrowed and heated, momentarily lost in his languorous gaze. I snapped my fingers in front of his face, grabbing his attention back up at my eyes. "Right." He chuckled with that sexy grin. "To make a long story short, Sicily and Marcus hooked up the first month, if not week, we were living together, and married two years into college. Which, sadly, has now come to an end. I'm here to represent her in the divorce and get a few financial things handled for her, as well as lend her support and a shoulder to cry on."

So Adam was not only gorgeous and sexy as all sin, he was a good guy, too; a good friend. Hmm. "What about her husband?" I questioned. "This has to make for an awkward situation, and cause resentment. Weren't you friends, too?"

"Roommates; not so much friends," Adam replied. "He hated that Sicily and I were close."

"Yeah," I giggled, "I bet he did. What man in his right mind would want his girl sharing time with the likes of you? It'd have to zap the ego." And logically, I couldn't see how any woman would pass on a chance to be with Adam, at least just once, and choose to just be friends. That made no sense whatsoever. Besides for the gorgeous looks, his charm and charisma suck you right in and intoxicate the senses. *Well, at least they do me.* How could you be near him and not be utterly spellbound.

"Marcus has ego to spare. The idiot," Adam snarled. "Sicily's expecting their first child. When he found out last month, that's what brought the divorce on. The slimy, jackass bastard decided he wasn't up for the challenge of a child, he's still one himself. My PI found he's had a couple of girlfriends on the side for the past year; something I didn't relish having to tell my friend Sicily about. But it gives leverage for us to stick it to him in the divorce."

Hmm.

"Enough serious talk," insisted Adam, reaching for the champagne bottle to top off our glasses. "Drink. And tell me about you; how long are you in Toronto for?" He pulled another chunk from the cake and moved to follow up my sip of champagne with it.

I'd hit my cake limit, so I held my hand up to stop him.

Adam threw back the piece himself. "How long, sweetheart?"

"Just long enough to give my pitch to the business group I'm meeting tomorrow, lunch, and fly out."

Adam didn't give a vocal response, just a slight nod of his head to acknowledge my words as he put his glass to his lips and drained the remains.

I shifted my naked self in my seat, sensing something was coming; he had that look in his eyes, all heated and gleaming. He was up to something naughty, and my insides twitched and cheered.

"Tell me, where's the craziest or most shocking place you've had sex?" he announced, his voice thick with huskiness.

And there it was.

"I fear I'm going to disappoint you, Mr. Blaire. I've never been very adventurous." It was the truth.

"What about sexual act?"

My cheeks flushed with heat. "The plane pleasure, today," I replied. *God, had that really happened? It seemed so unbelievable and surreal now, like a blissful blur. Dreamlike.*

"Me too; that definitely rates at the top for me," he said with a big ole sexy grin, adding, "Done anything like it before?"

"Of course not!"

"So I'm your first." Now I was grinning like a fool along with him; the way he'd said it, like a naughty statement, affirming, instead of a question. "Good," he murmured, "I'm glad I'm your first."

Me, too. But I didn't let Adam know that.

My fingers twined through my hair, absentmindedly gathering it over to one side, a mess of dark curls flowing over my breast and brushing my ribs.

"But the shower, backseat of a car…typical stuff?" he asked.

I nodded reluctantly. This was getting out of hand, and altogether too intimate. I was about to put a stop to it.

"With others around…in hearing range? Seeing range?"

What? Is he out of his mind? "I'm no exhibitionist, Mr. Blaire."

Adam's brow sexily cocked up. "How do you know, if you haven't tried?"

Well, he had a point. And I did enjoy the plane naughtiness.

That was spectacular. Still, that wasn't enough to convince me it was my thing.

"No kink at all?" Adam pressed.

I shook my head, "No." Though, my mind, *and my body*, were certainly more open to it now. Open to a bit of kink.

Adam's intense gaze burned through me, thinking of the possibilities.

I shifted in my seat again. *Was it me, or was it getting hot in here*?

My eyes followed as he leaned back and scooped his finger over the top of the cake, stealing a glob of chocolate fudge frosting. *I saw cake time*-slash-*get to know you time coming to an abrupt end*. Adam's whole upper body came at me from over the cake, catching his arm around the back of my waist and arching my chest to him. His eyes gleaming, Adam swiped frosting over one nipple and swirled it around the other, sure to include the fullness of my breast. The chocolaty finger slipped between my gaping lips and my mouth instinctively closed around his finger, sucking and tasting, tongue swirling away the remaining frosting.

I was stunned into submission as Adam dropped his head and took as much of my breast in his mouth as he could, doing some sucking and swirling of his own. I softly moaned out loud, arching into him even more, open and warm for him. His tongue glided across the valley between my breasts, swiping in a circular motion along the gentle slopes of each fleshy swell, licking up the frosting before his mouth opened up and clamped down on my nipple, pulling and sucking, teeth nipping and scraping... *Oh God*. My head fell back, blissful and agonizing sensations of pleasure spreading like wildfire throughout my body. I clasped onto Adam's shoulders, letting his arm at my back hold me up. He licked a trail up my throat, back to my mouth, drawing out a blazing passion. I was totally and completely drunk with lust for this man, my body aching, yearning...

Adam suddenly broke away, tugging at the cake tray and haphazardly setting it to the floor, clinking and clanging on his side of the bed, before leaning back to me with his hands high on my thighs, thumbs pressing into the hollows at my upper thighs and center; just as his mouth had earlier in the evening, beside the fire, when he'd purposely left his mark.

His mouth pressed back on mine, tongue delving in and possessing me while his body leaned on mine and pushed me back, forcing me down sideways on the bed; my legs still crossed like a pretzel, wide-open and exposed. Adam's thumbs kneaded and massaged, grazing at the wet readiness between my legs, a fleeting touch at my entrance, sending another rush of arousal and flood of heat. "Come here, you sexy thing," he growled, slipping me across the bed onto my side, spooning against him. One arm held me close, lying over my stomach while my head lay resting on the bicep of the other arm, my hand clasped in his…

Chapter Six

Adam's lips smoothed along my cheek laying soft kisses on my skin, his hardness pressing in from behind, perfectly snug between my butt cheeks as his fingers and thumb teased the delicate skin on my belly.

"You're an amazing woman, Bethany, and a marvelous lover. So willing, and responsive," he hummed along my ear, his lips gliding to my shoulder.

Hmm. Seems I am. That was a totally new revelation. No man had ever spoken such words to me before. I half wanted to cringe and turn inside myself with shameful shyness for what I'd done with this man...this sinfully *delicious* man...this stranger...how I'd '*responded*'. And half wanted to sit up and bang on my chest with pride, gorilla-style, brag and boast, and then run my tongue over and lick and taste and kiss every sweet morsel of Mr. Sinfully Sexy Man Candy pressed up behind me, and show him just how '*responsive*' I could be. Just how amazing of a lover I could be, and how in complete control of a man and his body I could be.

Yeah, that was new, too. But I did neither, of course.

Instead, I just let Adam's words sit a teeny minute.

His hand moved lower on my belly, holding me pressed to

him, his manhood deliciously rubbing against my backside as his lips affectionately peppered their way over the curve of my shoulder and down my arm. His fingers sashayed up my torso, giving attention to my left breast and then my right, while bestowing extra special devotion to my nipples. Bursts of raw pleasure once again shot through my veins.

When I just couldn't take the temptation at my backside any longer, I snuck my arm under Adam's and wedged it between us, my hand stealing a rousing feel over the ripples of hard ab muscles forming his glorious midsection, my fingers at last reaching the increasing hardness burning hot against my rear and gripping a hold with smooth strokes.

Adam gasped, the sudden, sharp intake of his breath pulsing against my back as the groan that followed rumbled in his chest and throbbed in my ear, vibrating through me.

It was such a beautiful, heady sound; *I* affected *him*—how about that! The mere thought sent desire ricocheting throughout my entire body.

Adam's hand moved from my breasts, danced across my abdomen and crept down my thigh, slipping to the inside of my knee and guiding my leg up over the outside of his, at his hip, opening me up for him. *I actually heard myself whimper in anticipation.* He let his fingers lazily slip between, tickling and teasing. I was still so sensitive; my body yet to fully recover from the multitude of torrents on the rug in front of the fire. One finger pushed in deeper, curling inside. "Seems that bit of rest did you good," Adam murmured thick and raspy, his tone oozing sex into my ear and eliciting a shiver that coursed down my spine.

I quickened my smooth strokes, gripping him tighter and keeping a steady rhythm.

Adam kissed his way back up my arm, his lips settling on the earlier mark of his passion, on the delicate skin at the bend of my neck and shoulder as his thumb pressed down on my sensitive sweet pearl, whispering and teasing out my inside secrets, euphoria glimmering on the horizon, bringing me toward sweet rapture.

Another whimper escaped and I squeezed Adam's hand tighter, squirming in pleasure under his touch. The tip of his nose brushed along the nape of my neck, scattering kisses as he went.

"I've never felt skin so soft," Adam passionately whispered his thought aloud.

I tensed, keenly aware this wasn't a normal response, at least not the one Adam probably expected with his whispered compliment. "I find that hard to believe, looking like you do, and having the skills that you do to back it up."

All kisses stopped. "So that makes me a liar?" Adam snapped in defense.

"No, just a charming player." *Not getting sucked into that. Again.*

"You wound me." He not so gently bit my shoulder, possibly trying to wound me in return, and then swirled his tongue over it.

I imagined the taste of my own flesh as Adam's tongue flirted with my skin, salty from sensual, sweaty sex—

"In case you're wondering," Adam broke into my imagining, "your skin is not only soft as a velvety rose petal, but tastes of heavenly sweetness, with a dash of saltiness sprinkled in." His tongue dipped behind my ear, dragging under my jaw, to the base of my neck on my collarbone, desire unfurling within.

Oh my. Not only does Adam read my body like he owns it, but my thoughts are his as well.

His hand between my legs nudged me back against him, at the same moment his hips thrust forward, stilling my hand gripping him between us.

"Damn, you feel so good," Adam growled, my own moan striking the air as liquid heat once more pooled at my sensitized core, responding to his words and touch. "And what you're doing to me with that hand…"

I tipped my head up and then back slightly, to gaze into his eyes, Adam's lips instead catching mine, claiming me as he does with exploding passion, our tongues a delicious tangling among whimpers and moans.

Adam broke away first, rolling onto his back and taking me with him, the back of my body lying flush on his chest and stomach, melding me to him while his fingers continued to tease and stroke, his other arm laying gently between my breasts with his fingers possessively on my collarbone.

I settled my head beside Adam's, resting on the curve of his neck and shoulder, my cheek smoothing his.

He pushed a finger inside, and my breath momentarily hitched at the surprise.

"Something new you want to do, or try? Maybe something wicked and kinky?" Adam sexily murmured. "Or are you content where we are, on this bed?"

Without hesitation, I released my bottom lip from between my teeth, not even realizing I'd been biting it, and let loose my reply, "To the floor to ceiling window."

"Aw...gotcha." Both of Adam's arms hugged around me, a pleased smile evident in his tone. "Drapes open, I assume? Balcony, maybe?" he questioned, trying to urge a little more out of me.

A flash of heat hit my cheeks. "No," I murmured softly. "Just the window, please." Ugh! Why was I suddenly feeling so shy and awkward about telling Adam what I wanted...?

Because I have no experience in doing so, maybe, that's why!

And then there was that come-hither finger inside me. "Behind, while I, um...look out at the view, watching city life moving and hustling about in the twinkling evening lights, unaware." And our reflection playing out in front of me.

"Get your heels on."

Ooh. I think I loved that idea even more than Adam visibly did.

He hauled me to my feet and I scurried about the suite, in search of where we'd flung my heels in our earlier frenzy.

In nothing but my nakedness and my high-heeled slingbacks, I hurried back to Adam; lights still dimmed, candlelight and firelight still flickering and glowing about the room as he drew the drapes open, unveiling the expansive wall of windows and the spectacular cityscape beyond.

Adam turned when he felt me nearing, pausing to take in the sight before him. Those beautiful sea blue eyes, lazy and heated, grazed over me head to toes, settling on my feet with rapt appreciation for the crimson heels he'd requested I slip back into. "Sweetheart, you are a vision," he rasped. "Every man's erotic fantasy." His hand reached out for mine, and I took a couple steps closer, slipping my fingers into the palm of his proffered hand.

Adam swiftly yanked me in to his chest, and I squealed in surprise, his arm coming around me as his hand found the back of my jaw, his lips gently brushing over mine while his massive body acted like a protective wall of muscle, shielding sight of me from outside the window.

His fingers fiddled with something behind my back and in the same moment bright light flickered on around us, ensuring the thrill of being seen, the entire bedroom lit up. *Slick...the lights operate by remote.* Adam quickly tossed the remote aside, landing it in a corner chair.

"Are you ready," he murmured, his lips playing at the bottom edge of my lip, and corner.

I nodded my head with certainty and Adam spun us, flipping our positions in front of the window, my bare backside now on full display.

I right away dropped to me knees before him, ready to do a little pleasure reciprocating; payback for the multiple 'O's in front of the fire.

Adam's eyes grew wide, "Not necessary."

I stared up at him, batting my lashes and licking my lips, hoping to look all sexy and seductive. "Just a taste...please?"

Adam gasped. "Aw, hell, Bethany."

He wasn't the only one shocked. I'd never felt the urge before; especially never so strongly. It's not something I found pleasureble; in truth, I found it demeaning—on my knees servicing a man like a whore. In fact, my last relationship, it never happened once. *Huh. Maybe that should have been a clue.*

Adam had stirred some kind of sexual awakening—unleashed the beast within. Now it seemed like the best damn thing *ever*, getting down on my knees before Adam; something I'd thoroughly enjoy, and craved with every cell of my being; like I'd die if I didn't have him between my lips in the next few seconds, for my own pleasure as well as pleasuring Adam.

"A taste," Adam suddenly groaned, need and want spilling from his words and spiraling inside me, sending my own desire escalating. *Mmm...* Which encouraged me that much more. I ran my hands slowly up his strong thighs, resting them close on either side of my target. There was no need for my hands to guide him;

he was marvelously lifted to attention.

Adam stroked the length of my hair with his hands; not a tight grasp or push, just gentle strokes. *Until...*

My lips touched the base, spreading soft kisses lightly up—warmth and exhilaration tingling on my lips—and gliding my tongue back down.

...both of Adam's hands shot up and hit splayed out on the window.

"Oh God—F...you can't do that!" Adam blew out in a rush, groaning low and deep as he jerked beneath my tongue.

My lashes fluttered up at him. "God, has nothing to do with it," I was quick to sassily quip back.

Adam's hands slapped on my upper arms and he yanked me up—eyes dark, lusty and heated, locked on mine with blazing passion. "There are no words, baby—" he exhaled, "I won't last."

Really? I thought briefly. *Mr. Always Ready*?

Adam's kiss was hot and needy, his hands greedy and grasping on my nipples and breasts.

He whirled me around, facing away from him, my arms stretched out quick above my head, hands spread on the cold glass window as he roughly kicked my feet apart, my heels skittering across the carpet.

The city lit up beneath the night sky, stars magnificently twinkling and shimmering in front of me, Adam blanketed me with the heat of his bare body, sandwiching me against the glass. The backs of his fingers brushed up my sides, his hands moving up my arms and covering my hands. "Have you done this before?" he softly whispered on my ear.

"Wh—What?" I stammered, taken completely off guard by Adam's question, unable to concentrate on anything other than his hot, rock hard body pressed against my backside and my boobs smushed against the window.

"The window," he whispered again "...in view...the possibility of being seen?"

I was pretty sure it was too far up to clearly be seen...well, at least not without a fine pair of binoculars. I answered simply, "No."

"Good." Adam breathed in deeply, gliding his nose through

my hair and taking in the scent. "Glad I'm you're first."

Mmm…Me, too.

And then he switched gears, his hand coming down fast and pushing on my lower belly, forcing my ass to stick out toward him as a sudden sting struck one butt cheek and then the other, fire striking quick and zinging to my core. I shrieked, realization dawning on me that Adam had spanked me, the sting coming from his hand cracking against my ass. But just as swift, his hands were caressing and massaging each cheek, thumbs running hot up between—Whoa!—to the forbidden zone.

Passionate lips fixed on my upper back, my hair falling forward.

He kept one distracting hand firm on the curve of my hip while the other wicked hand reached between my legs from behind, his middle finger stealing a swipe through my slick heat and taking a dip.

"Mmmmm," Adam hummed his pleasure, his breath hot on my neck, "Bless you."

I assumed he meant that I was wet and ready for him.

Adam's hand left from underneath, reaching around my hip to the front of me and finding the pearly bud he was after, ready to release the magic while he plunged into me from behind. "Fu…" he roughly gasped, "give me a second, please?" stilling there inside me, my bare ass still pushed out flush against him.

I got the feeling he was trying to take it slow and steady, to maybe enjoy our moment unhurried and make it last. *Hmph.* I snickered inside. *Not happening.* "Adam—" I hardly recognized my own voice, thick with lust, all sexy and wanton, "—think we can do this hard and rough, this time?" Okay, forget not recognizing my own voice… Who the hell was this woman? I never ask for it… Especially hard!

Adam slapped my ass cheek again, "*Hell yeah*, sweetheart," and I clenched tight around him, hit with a rush of arousal. He grasped a hand back on my hip and another between my shoulder blades, pushing me down and holding me in place as he pulled back slowly.

I braced myself against the window, ready to take all that Adam was about to give—to get what I asked for.

But he surprised me, slowly trailing his finger from the nape of my neck down the center of my back, softly caressing each hill and valley along my spine. Then he dragged his tongue along the same path, sensuously gliding it across my skin. When he reached the base of my spine, he placed a tender kiss to each of my lower back dimples, my body shuddering under his gentle touch.

In the full light of the bedroom, highlighting reality—city twinkling and starlight sparkling in front of us, anticipation and desire zinging throughout and lighting a fire within—Adam slammed into me. A resounding grunt echoed through the suite, hushing my own cry, Adam driving into me over and over and over again: hips slapping, slapping hard, skin on skin. There was nothing gentle or sweet about it; it was full on taking and claiming, with audible groans, grunts, and moans.

The beautiful sounds of our pleasure filling my ears, I dazed out, absorbing it all, for a split second focusing on the world outside the floor to ceiling wall of windows, suddenly struck with the height. It was somewhat dizzying, being so high up, ironically just as Adam was about to take me even higher, with an exhilarating plummet over the edge. *Just the thought was enough to take me over that edge.*

His hand left my back and his fingers threaded through the nape of my hair, forcefully yanking my head. I cried out, pain tingling throughout my scalp and shooting straight to the tiny bundle of nerves in the sweetest spot, eliciting a pleasurable pain I hadn't known existed.

And Adam knew it, tugging that fistful full of hair a little harder, his brutal thrusts coming quicker. "Look out the window," he growled in demand, "not at what's happening down below, but straight out ahead." I dragged my gaze upwards. "See those dim lights, and those silhouettes? At least sixty separate windows, all possibly watching, enthralled with the pleasure on your beautiful face, waiting—spiraling along with you—for the moment heaven falls over you."

I was sure I'd never heard a sexier voice in all my life.

I moaned louder, focusing on those room windows across from us, the thought of being watched thrilling the bare skin of my body, my every nerve on fire, almost sending me over. I pawed at the window, Adam's panting breaths pulsing behind me. He released my hair, his hand gripping onto my bare hip, moving at a furious pace with fierce, demanding passion.

I caught a glimpse of Adam's reflection just then, the lit up windows beyond falling out of focus and the intense desire on Adam's face suddenly prominent as he devoured me—I could no longer tell where his body stopped and mine started, disappearing into me as he was. The unbearably sweet friction between us...it was so much more than I'd bargained for when I'd said *yes* to tonight.

I pushed back, grinding into him even more, his thrusts reaching in and touching deeper and deeper, seeking out and rubbing and stroking my most intimate parts, revealing secrets that had long ago been tucked and hidden away, waiting to be found.

Waiting for Adam, *the pleasure whisperer*.

My legs started to shake, my body trembling and my inside nerves bundling and exquisitely tightening as my hands began to slip on the glass. Adam's sweaty palms assured their grip on my equally-sweaty hips, my legs about to give out and his hands on my hips the only thing holding me up.

One more delicious drive, deep—

Oh. My. God!

—And he hit the mark!

My body bolted upright, crashing against Adam's chest, my arms reaching up behind me and cinching around the back of Adam's neck. His hands clamped onto my breasts, aggressively working their magic as my hair fell wild over my shoulders, sticking to the side of my face, Adam's chest, and his arms in the sweaty heat of the moment. Adam used his chin to swipe the hair away from my face, one hand skimming down my stomach to the delicate bundle of magic and warmth below, fingers swirling a smooth rhythm of frenzied circles.

"Yes!" I cried out—*Oh my God, yes*!—pressing my head back on Adam's shoulder as the night exploded!

Adam crushed his mouth to mine, claiming my mouth like he was claiming my release...hard and rough like I'd asked. "Look at me!" he ordered, and my pinched eyelids immediately sprang open, his command snapping my gaze up to him.

One more sharp strike and Adam was chasing after me, pulsing and throbbing, his body shuddering against mine. His arms tightened around my middle as he folded me over, riding out the remains of our releases, my hands reaching for purchase on the back of his thighs.

It was insane, what this man could do to my body, how he made me feel. I was a quivering, shaking, trembling hot mess.

But deliciously, deliriously pleasured.

I could very easily become addicted to this, this feeling, this heightened level of delirious pleasure, and, dare I say…this man.

One night, Beth, one night!

He's just like the rest—though more charming and infinitely better looking than most men, still incapable of being satisfied with one woman for very long.

Our sweaty bodies melded together, both speechless, Adam somehow summoned the strength to get us back to the bed; my entire body rendered the consistency of Jell-O by our doings, and my eyelids fluttering, begging to close for a few minutes…*or hours!*

We collapsed in a tangled heap of skin, my hair again flowing over us, threatening to stick to our sopping wet skin. *Mmmm, sweet sweet afterglow.*

"A million times over I could watch you," Adam murmured, repeating his earlier remark, his body twisted around mine in the center of the large bed, holding me tight within his arms. He reverently kissed the top of my head.

Little bells of warning alarmed, flickering thoughts of reason about the coziness of our mingling, but I brushed them aside…all in for the one night stand experience…letting myself go, and opening up.

"So damn lucky…" Adam panted, chest heaving heavy from exertion. I wondered for a minute what he meant. He continued on, his fingers casually tracing circles on my naked hip, "Lucky to be doubly fortunate today… First—"

I giggled inside, Mr. Sex God here, was trying desperately to control his breathing and get out the words to express his thought, but struggling miserably. I placed my palm on his chest, and felt the immediate stutter of his heart and pause in breath. The next breath he took was calmer, his hand stroking over the top of mine.

"...First, that you chose to fly first class today—"

I focused on our hands, the way his much larger hand consumed mine, his fingers curled into my palm as his thumb rubbed back and forth over the top.

"Second, that your last partner chose to be an idiot bastard, foolish enough to not see what a freaking beautiful, *hot* goddess you are. A rare jewel. And more importantly, that you chose to wear that figure hugging skirt, without panties." He playfully swatted my naked behind, caressing his hand over afterwards. "Bless you for that, sweetheart. I can't say it enough."

I was fairly certain I was the lucky one, *my body had never known such pleasure*, but I kept that little tidbit to myself. Who was I to disagree with him, Mr. Almighty Powerful Sex God?

"Lastly, I'd be remiss if I didn't give thanks to your friend—Lizzy, was it?—for kicking you toward me, and suggesting you shake it up." *Yeah, I owe her for that little nudge, myself; I would not be here without it.* "Please, do make sure you thank her for me." His fingers slipped under my chin and led my gaze up to him.

Those eyes, there was that lustful, heated look again in that beautiful, intense sea blue. For a second, I thought I felt a tiny spark down below, in effect—in my nether regions—but it was too weak to be certain.

"Thank you for this night," Adam whispered. He met his lips softly to mine, his tongue gently parting my lips and sliding in, stroking my tongue with his tender touch. *Yep.* That was definitely a spark below, and it felt a little stronger this time, teasing the flame of desire.

I felt a warm flush bloom on my cheeks and spread down my throat, to my chest. *What is it about this man?* His fingers slipped to the small of my back, nestling me in a bit closer.

Truthfully, if I got any closer, I'd be on top of him. My body couldn't possibly take him again, of that I felt fairly certain. But the evidence of his arousal rubbing against me, was tempting me to reconsider. *Demanding it.* Adam clearly had other ideas; he didn't appear to be slowing down yet...

He ran a hand over my hip and down the side of my leg. "So silky soft," he murmured, his hand slipping to the inside of my knees and smoothing its way up. "Think maybe I can sling this soft, feminine body of yours over one of those black velvet armchairs, and take you another time?"

The thought of my '*soft, feminine body*' accepting him one more time, bent over that chair... Mercy, I already knew I'd let him, regardless of how spent my body was and how sore and achy I was feeling, it was something I was willing to try... *needed* to try.

Lying lazily in the afterglow, Adam's body twined with mine after yet another round of commingling and an amazing, mind-blowing, toe curling series of epic releases—this time with my hands gripped on the headboard as Adam rocked below me, after first trying out that black velvet armchair, my body slung over one arm being taken hard from behind—with complete unawareness, sleep finally took us...

Chapter Seven

Weary as I was, I must've dozed off, next thing I knew I awoke to the sound of running water, still in a bit of a champagne haze. I dreamily blinked up to see Adam standing over me. "Morning, Sunshine," he murmured cheerily, giving me pause. *Morning*?

I slept all night?

I sleepily said, "Morning, already?" followed with a yawn.

Adam chuckled softly. "Technically, yes, it's 2:30 A.M.." He scooped me from the bed and took me to the bathroom, the tub to be specific.

Sheesh, can't a girl get some sleep after being sinfully ravished and pleasurably used?

"I...I couldn't...possibly..." Could I? Could my body accept Adam one more time?

Of all the men to pick for a casual one night stand, I choose Mr. Energizer Bunny...with enough stamina for ten men... A stallion.

"The tub will help soothe your soreness." There he went again, reading my thought before I could put it into speakable words. And, *wow*, he was looking pretty gorgeous; his hair all sexily mussed, and his voice all sexily gruff.

The large Jacuzzi tub was already filled; bath salts added and pale purple bubbles floating, the bathroom smelling gloriously of lavender.

Adam tipped my feet to the water and set me down, the warm water and soothing jets calling me into it. I cautiously sank beneath the bubbles, the pulsating jets soothing me at once.

My stomach suddenly tightened, realizing Adam was standing beside the tub, *naked*. Holy Hell! Was he getting in with me? That was…would be…entirely too intimate.

"Relax," he intuitively spoke. "I don't have to join you; I already showered." I anxiously worked my bottom lip between my teeth—of course, while lingeringly skimming my gaze over Adam's manly rock hard body, all his delicious nakedness, pausing impolitely too long on his manhood; *Jesus the man was perfect!*—feeling uneasy about this whole scene. What was Adam up to? I mean, really, I was perfectly content, sleeping soundly. What possessed him to wake me? For what, a bath? What was the hurry? I could run through a quick shower in the morning, before my meeting. *Ugh, my meeting.* Being at the top of my game with so little sleep…I was hoping it wouldn't prove to be an issue. This account's too important…*and huge.*

Speaking of huge… My naked sex god was leaning over the tub, squirting body wash into a deep purple shower pouf and lathering it up. Uh, was he planning to wash me…? I was plenty capable myself, and up for the task. I reached for the pouf, but Adam was too quick. "Let me." His eyes sparkled, and a sweet smile followed, rendering me immobile.

"I need to sleep… Awww—" He held my hand and glided the spongy pouf from my shoulder down my arm in gentle, circular motions, his fingers laced between mine. With a blissful sigh, my head settled onto the comfy tub pillow. Heavenly.

"I know you're tired, baby," his murmured words fell over me, his lips touching softly on my forehead. My eyes dreamily fluttered open. "But you needed to wash—"

"What was the rush?" My pulsed quickened, the body pouf touching to the side of my neck and gliding along my collarbone, motioning down my chest.

Adam's lips brushed the top curl of my ear, "Your scent," he whispered seductively, licking and kissing his way to my earlobe.

"You're altogether too intoxicating, sweetheart. I wasn't about to send you off to your meeting, where I assume there will be other men in attendance, smelling as you do. Of sex."

Whoa! Okay, that was odd. *Weird* even. What did he care? "Adam—"

"Shhh," he hummed on my earlobe, a finger gently pressed on my lips. "Would you consider staying another night?"

Wh—What? The. Hell. "No."

And that was the last word, Adam's fingers curling behind my left knee as he lifted my leg to him, successfully parting my legs as he set the soapy pouf in motion...

~ * ~

I awoke before my scheduled wakeup call, ensnared in a web of Adam's limbs, a melded twist of heated skin. He had a leg between mine, hooked behind my knee and stuck to my calf. His one arm supported my head between his chest, shoulder and bicep, while the lower portion of that same arm was wedged underneath mine at my side, with his hand cupping the entirety of one breast. Adam's other hand, no surprise, was perfectly seated on my ass. And his magnificent manhood, yet again fully aroused, was pressed on my lower belly, nuzzling into my belly-button. *I was tempted to take care of that.* The man was sexy as sin, and hot as hell—I mean literally, my skin was on fire against his.

I took the opportunity, while Adam couldn't catch me, to let my naughty eyes roam. I drank in the sight of him, of us, all twisted together, fully exposed with the bedding wadded in a bundle at the foot of the enormous bed, firelight still faintly flickering about. He was quite a sight; all perfect features, hard muscle and tanned skin. *Shame I wouldn't have the opportunity to appreciate any of it again, all that remarkable perfection.* I listened to Adam's shallow breathing for a few minutes. Assured he was sleeping soundly, I gingerly snuck from his arms, curled away from his body, then stole from bed. Right away wincing... *Wow, were my muscles sore. Parts I hadn't even known could hurt, were in pain—the delicious sort of pain, that is.*

I squinted my eyes slightly. *By some small miracle, I had only a mild headache; far better than I deserved, for all the champagne I drank with Adam last night*. The drapes were still open on the expansive window, and early morning light flooded in. Gloomy as usual. It was fitting though; it kind of fit my mood. And peeking out from all that gloom, was a tiny sliver of sunshine, a tease of the possibility of a brighter day ahead.

A fleeting visual of what we'd done in front of that window came whirling into memory— My body pressed to that window, hands splayed on the glass, legs spread apart wide, Adam hard and rough between, the thrill of being seen, and watched... *Wow*! That'd get me nowhere, thoughts like that.

I set to quickly gathering my things—plucking yesterday's clothes up from the floor, having been carelessly strewn about in our frenzy last night—and readying myself, hoping to sneak out before Adam woke. *I know, cowardly.* I stuffed yesterday's clothes in my bag, then slipped into the peacock blue skirt and sleeveless, black silk blouse I'd brought to wear for today's meeting. I saved the coordinating suit jacket to shimmy into when I was about to scoot out the door. Then I set my luggage and things beside the doorway into the master suite, ready to make my speedy exit, and then strode off to the bathroom with my toiletries in hand.

I washed my face, brushed my teeth and applied my makeup in record time. I was thankful Adam had the foresight to get bathing out of the way last night...well, technically it was earlier this morning. I felt he'd given me a better chance of slipping out of the suite without notice, or waking him—if only he'd known.

I whipped my long, dark hair into a smooth twist and pinned it into place, lacquering it up with a finishing spray and piecing out a few messy tendrils of loose curls, to avoid a too done up look. All I needed was a touch of color and gloss on my lips. I searched my makeup bag for the sheer lip gloss I'd tossed in before I'd left home.

I felt before I saw; an electric charge shot down my spine and I gave a startled jump, two strong arms coming around my waist from behind and pulling me close into a warm, hard body—I should add that that body was *naked*!—a chin resting on my shoulder.

"Going somewhere?" soft lips sternly whispered hot at my ear; beautiful, smoldering, blue-green bedroom eyes fixed on mine in the mirror.

I was too stunned to speak. Quick fingers deftly tugged at the bottom of my blouse, freeing it from the waistband of my skirt and sashaying underneath the hemline, fast under my lacy bra cup. I gasped a sharp intake of breath, my breath releasing in a moan. *Holy hell*! My skirt was inching up. *Snap out of it Beth*! I pulled myself from my dreamy state and somehow escaped Adam's hold. *Christ, if his effect wasn't fast*. I bolted out of his reach, standing staring at him—like the proverbial deer in the headlights—a few feet away, plastered against the wall. *Damn sexy man*. How was it possible for a man to wake up looking so damn gorgeous and yummy? His hair was sexily mussed and tousled, standing there in a confident stance with his arms crossed over his chest, naked and *ready* for me. *Mercy*!

My eyes rested on his face. His eyes held a note of...*hmm* ...sadness under that smoldering gaze. His handsome face, now scruffy and sexy, somehow looked even better than it had yesterday, clean shaven... *Sexier*! And his deep, raspy morning voice... did unspeakable things to me.

Oh, how I wanted to melt into that body for eternity... *Or at least for a little while longer*.

He took a step nearer, briefly drawing my gaze to his bare feet. *Lord, even his feet were sexy*.

I tried to sidestep around him to escape the bathroom, but Adam was quick to block me.

"Stay another night with me," he said. It wasn't a question, more a statement, a sort of demand.

My gaze snapped back up to him. "I fly out later today, following my meeting."

"Please." He lunged at me, and I stealthily snatched my toiletry bag and dodged around him, successfully escaping the confines of the bathroom, en route to the bedroom doorway and my things. I snatched my carryon suitcase and saddled my laptop-*slash*-briefcase on top of it, clasping my purse in my other hand.

Adam was hot on my trail, still trying to convince me.

I speedily slipped into my high heels, and kept moving. "Let's not make more of this than it is, Adam. We both knew going in that it was just one night, that was 'the deal'."

"Deals are meant to be broken—"

"Don't go getting all lawyerly on me."

It wasn't going to end well anyway; at least not for me. A man like Adam would never settle for, or be happy with, one woman, especially not me. Might as well save myself the heartache and end it now. That's exactly why I swore off men two months ago …to avoid the heartache, at the inevitable end.

I reached the doorway, luggage in hand. "Goodbye, Mr. Blaire."

Adam grabbed my arm from behind me, "Change your flight. Stay another night with me? After your meeting we can… I can take advantage of you all day and night."

"Jesus," I muttered under my breath, shaking my head as I whirled my body around to face him, my arms crossed determinedly in front of me. "I agreed to one night, Mr. Blaire," I reminded him, "I have a business to get back to." Honestly, that raspy, pleading voice coming from that still naked, gorgeous, hot man was getting to me. I was wishing he'd put some damn clothes on, to make it easier on me and help me keep my resolve …well, just half-heartedly wishing. Might as well get my fill.

"Just kiss me goodbye, Adam."

"I don't want to." I giggled inside. He sounded like a petulant, pouting child. "I don't want you to go. Not yet."

I cocked a brow at him. "Aren't you the one with experience in hookups, no strings attached?"

Adam narrowed his gaze and frowned.

"Just one night, that was *the deal*, Adam."

"Let me get dressed," he snarled, "I'll walk you down." He plucked his slacks and crumpled dress shirt from the floor where they were flung during last night's frenzied passion.

"That's not necessary."

He shimmied into his slacks. "I'm not letting you just—"

"One night, Adam, that was *the deal*." Damn it!

His shirt was next. "I'm walking you out Bethany," he gritted out, haphazardly buttoning shirt buttons. "Though, I see nothing wrong with a two night stand."

"I'm sure you can find a willing female body to spread your hotness on this weekend."

"Yours is the only body I'd like to spread my 'hotness' on," he rasped. "Preferably every sinfully sweet square inch of you."

Ooh. My insides clenched. *I'd like that, too.* But, lest I forget, this man could break my heart in the blink of an eye.

Not bothering to find his shoes, Adam met me at the main door into the suite, gesturing to the handle of my bag to gentlemanly relieve the burden of me pulling it myself. "I got it," I snapped firmly, tugging it ahead while he held the door open.

Adam shook his head in irritation. "Are you always this stubborn?"

"If by '*stubborn*' you mean independent, then yes." I strode ahead with my baggage in tow. Adam followed a few steps behind with his sullen mood. I wondered what was up with the mood. He'd been so cheery from the moment he entered that air cabin.

And there we were again, awkwardly standing before the elevator, waiting for the doors to open. I pressed the call button a second time, praying for the damn thing to hurry the hell up already! The charge from Adam's nearness, the aching need for his touch and skin tingling exhilaration, was driving me wild with desire. *I'd never felt such strong desire, such longing.* But Adam kept his hands to himself, seeming to have finally gotten the message...the fun was over.

The elevator doors parted, and in I went, right away to the left side wall, again. Only this time Adam shadowed me, moving in close and pressing me to the cool elevator wall, the handrail at my rear.

I blinked up at him, his dark gaze staring down at me. *Oh, my.* I wondered why his chest was heaving so.

But, then again, mine was too.

His thumb gently traced the fullness of my bottom lip, leaving a searing trail of fire on its way to my top lip. His tongue darted out, his hips giving a little grind against me. "So this is it?" he asked as he pushed his thumb into my mouth and ran it along the inside of my bottom lip.

I nodded my head slightly. *Mercy.* All I could think about was the contact of those hips, in conjunction with the stimulating sensation of that thumb in my mouth.

Adam's head tipped in acquiescence, and then dropped down, angling slightly as his lips met mine. Slow at first, soft and sweet, moving in deeper, his tongue sensuously caressing mine.

I was a goner.

My hand flew into his rumpled and tousled hair, mussing it a bit more while I held him to me, insuring that kiss would linger and last.

A low groan rose from Adam's throat, passing to me in a mouth sweeping hum, and I softly whimpered... *The man could kiss*!

Girly giggles rang out in the elevator. Only then did I realize we weren't alone in the elevator-*slash*-hot box of lust.

I felt Adam's smile, and the pulse of breath from his chuckle.

He playfully teased my bottom lip and drew it between his lips, teeth grazing and nipping, before completely pulling back, his hips still pressed against me, pinning me, making sure I felt the evidence of his desire for me.

Trust me, it was hard to miss.

"You put on a good show, Bethany," he teased, a bit of a laugh sneaking out, amused that we'd had an audience.

I slapped my hands against the hard planes of his chest and pushed him back. "Me?" I frowned. "You initiated that kiss, Mr. Blaire."

I noted the two teenage girls huddled together in the corner, still in a fit of giggles.

Thank goodness the elevator doors opened.

The girls fled, amidst peals of laughter as they exited into the grand hotel lobby.

Perfect. I hated being a spectacle.

Adam didn't give me a chance to grab my bag this time, his hand beating me to the handle. He slipped his other hand into mine, his large fingers lacing between my much smaller ones, holding my hand as we stepped over the threshold, headed toward the lobby.

The sexy fool certainly had a sweet side. The way he adoringly held my hand, like he'd done it for years, and feared—

"I can't get enough of you; I'm like a starved man near you."

My belly churned with desire, suddenly ravenous…for Adam!

Maybe it was better this way, leaving with the truest feeling of what real, raw desire felt like. To at least once in my life know it, know the intense need and passionate feeling, and remember it. To know I'd had it…felt it…and that it existed. Without the devastatingly shattered, broken heart, when it inevitably ended.

I clung onto that thought to help summon the will to say good-bye.

"Screw this! Once more," Adam fervently blurted, his voice coated thick with desire, yanking me by the hand back into the elevator, luggage wheels skidding along behind. He at once hit the close door button, setting the elevator in motion, and then just as quickly slammed his palm against the red emergency stop button, abruptly halting the elevator between floors one and two with a jarring jolt. I wanted to protest, but the words just weren't there.

My heart thudded in my chest, but it was brief, Adam was on me in a second's time, owning me with his kiss, my heart pounding and racing like wildfire as his tongue did amazing things in my mouth. I was hauled up to the elevator wall above the handrail in the same frenzy as we'd entered our suite the night before. Adam's hand snaked its way onto my naked hip as I was barely aware of my skirt bunching up around my waist, freeing my legs to twist around Adam.

"Fuck, I love that you're always ready; no panties in the way," he hissed. "I'd have ripped the damn things off anyway." His hand slipped fast between my thighs from my backside, two fingers plunging inside as his mouth made sensual, sexy love with mine, wholly possessing me. *My mouth would forever feel Adam's taste, my body his touch. I was sure of it.* Adam's fingers were suddenly gone, his wrist pressed and wiggling against my delicate flesh as he loosened the button and zipper on his slacks, trailing with the swift tear of a packet. And—*We both gasped.*—I was once again filled, fuller and deeper, a slow rocking at first and then the full, hard, fast thrust of Adam's hips, bringing the quick accumulation of our releases to a fervent, explosive completion, my release followed by Adam's, moaning in unison as I clawed at his back and dug my heels into his magnificent backside.

Ahhhh…the man was breathtaking. His lips slowed on mine, nipping at the plumpness of my kiss swollen bottom lip, and then my chin. His tongue slid down my throat, his fingers working on the first few buttons on my blouse. "Oh, what you do to me." His hand slipped in, and his tongue followed.

Oh. My. God.

I found myself grasping onto the back of Adam's head, greedily pushing him down on my breast. He bit and teased my nipple, swirling his tongue and sucking mercilessly on the sensitive tip between bites. He was relentless. One finger tenderly circled my opening, gently entering, mimicking the rhythm and strokes of his tongue. All be damned if he didn't bring on another one, my body shuddering softly, Adam's finger wringing out every last, blissful spasm. I quivered in his arms, clamping my hands on either side of his fabulous face and bringing those lips to me. This time, *I* kissed *him.*

It was my goodbye.

I wiggled my skirt back in place as my backside slid down from the elevator wall and the souls of my peacock blue high heels touched back to reality, released from the strong arms that held me. Adam tapped the tip of one finger on the emergency stop button, resuming our descent in the elevator, and then got down to the business of handling his issues below the waist.

I snuck a quick peek at my reflection in one of the mirrored elevator walls, my fingers frantically taming my hair and tugging at my shirt buttons, hoping to hide the fact that I'd just been thoroughly ravished in the elevator.

In mere seconds the doors were opening and we were again forced to step out of the elevator. We sauntered toward the lobby without words, my luggage in tow.

Adam saw me through the grand entrance-*slash*-exit doors of the hotel, my town car awaiting me.

I turned to him, "Goodbye, Adam." *Okay. Why was my voice so shaky?* He blinked down at me, taking pause, and then lunged at me with one last kiss, soft and bittersweet, his fingers clasped on the back of my jaw.

I opened up for him, letting him slide his tongue along mine, one last time, feeling the gentle tug inside as our tongues passionately danced, raising goose bumps across my skin.

"Promise me one thing…" Adam whispered on my lips. "You won't make a habit of this one night stand thing." *Seriously?* "Not every man's going to treat you like I did. Stay sworn off men till you find the right one." He disarmingly looked into my eyes, seeking assurance.

That realization had already occurred to me—that's likely why I was so able to give so much of myself, and open myself up; the level of trust Adam compelled, and the type of man he was—there would never be another night like the one I shared with Adam. All others would be mere hookups; going through the motions with weak satisfaction, and little to no desire. My head slightly nodded in recognition, and Adam brushed a slow kiss on my forehead.

My damn knees were wobbling. *Keep it together Beth. Think like a man.*

I murmured once more, "Goodbye, Adam. Thanks for the memorable night." I winked at him. *And the most sinfully erotic night of my life!* "It was nice meeting you, Mr. Blaire."

"The pleasure was all mine, sweetheart." One corner of his mouth curled up into the playful, sexy grin I'd already learned to know and love. *He really was quite charming.*

The driver loaded my carryon luggage into the trunk of the car. I kept my handbag and laptop in hold. Adam stood at the door as I slipped into the backseat, and then stepped back when the driver came back and closed the door between us.

The windows were tinted too dark for Adam to see me, but my view of him was still perfect. He hadn't moved but a couple of feet back.

As the driver pulled ahead, I watched Adam, somewhat of a lost-*slash*-pained expression on his devastatingly handsome face, his hands tucked into the front pockets on his slacks, beautifully barefoot, and the top couple buttons on his rumpled white dress shirt left casually undone, exposing a teasing peek at his sexy chest and a dusting of dark hair.

I unconsciously worked my bottom lip between my teeth.

Could the man be any sexier?
Lord.
This just might be the image of him I remember most fondly.

For a brief, flash of a moment, I thought to halt the driver so I could jump out and run back to Adam, to take him up on his offer of another night of passion, and wild sexcapades. *What would one more night hurt?*

But sense prevailed.

One night of blissful ecstasy was what I would have to look back on with the sexy Mr. Adam Blaire, knowing no other man would ever come close to bringing me such heavenly pleasure, nor have magic skills to compare… He had ruined me.

I turned back around in my seat and faced forward, closing my eyes as "Goodbye, Adam," softly whispered between my lips into the emptiness of the backseat.

I gave myself a couple minutes to pull myself together, before I reached for my laptop to review the presentation I was about to pitch the hotel board of executives, and get my head in the game. A little twinge of regret plagued me; not that I'd shared the night of sinfully wicked sex with Adam, but for declining his offer for a second night.

One thing was for sure, Adam wasn't kidding last night when he'd threatened… "I'm going to make damn sure you remember me with every step you take tomorrow, and very possibly clear into next week." I would *absolutely* be remembering him with my every step—I most certainly was now, with every movement. But my fear was that the rest of me—my mind, my body, and my very soul—would be remembering Adam and our night together for far beyond that. His touch, his taste, his voice…

We shared little words, in our night together, but somehow I still shared so much more of myself than I ever had with any other in my past.

And I'd most definitely experienced the best sex of my life. I never knew such ecstasy existed, or that I could open up and allow it. Adam had unleashed a level of passion and pleasure that never would compare and that I'd undoubtedly be unsuccessfully seeking for the rest of my life…

The man had wiggled his way under my skin.

Though, I was proud of myself; I'd pulled off one hell of a magnificent one night stand! With unequivocally the perfect man...

~ *The End* of '*First Sight: The Deal Prequel*' ~

For more of Adam and Bethany read their full story in '*The Deal*'~

'*The Deal*' *Brief Synopsis* ~

On a business flight from LAX to Toronto, Bethany Drake has the delightful, though unexpected, fortune of being seated next to gorgeous and boldly exciting Adam Blaire—the most sought after divorce attorney in Beverly Hills, with a steadfast belief against commitment and/or monogamy.

Bethany, a successful graphic designer with her own agency, has never been very successful in the relationship department, and her recent breakup has left her sworn off men. But the gorgeous man beside her draws her in, compels a trust in him that she just can't deny, and she throws caution to the wind.

After an illicit encounter midair, the two end up sharing a blissful night of ecstasy in a Toronto hotel suite, which leaves them with an appetite for each other, and a brainstorm…when neither is able to get the other out from under their skin.

The deal: 'Sex, devoid of any emotion or connection, other than pure, raw pleasure.

It seems a win-win.

They set to deliciously agreeing to the rules, while in bed, naked, armed with a tube of lipstick, chocolate sauce, and an iPad, for photographic proof. With a clear price set, the consequence, if emotions should come in to play… They'll simply walk away. Deal's off!

What they do not plan for, or expect, are the intimate moments that sneak in between the sex. The ease of comfort between them… The connection… Their soul deep need for the other…

The man simply nuzzles his way into every crevice of her life.

~ * ~

http://www.amazon.com/Deal-Deborah-Ann-ebook/dp/B00PLZRB31/

Print versions also available, on Amazon.com
http://www.amazon.com/Deborah-Ann/e/B009QQK471/

UK Site
http://www.amazon.co.uk/gp/product/B00FR0L8B8

The Deal

Chapter One ~ Excerpt

"So, we have a deal. Sex, devoid of any emotion or connection, other than pure, raw pleasure." He held his hand out to me, and I met my palm to his, to shake on it.

"Yep. That's the deal."

I met Adam last month on a business flight from LAX to Toronto; he, too, was traveling on business, and was seated beside me in first class. My initial impression of Adam, was that he was extremely good-looking—obvious to all upon seeing him, I was sure: classic Hollywood looks, dark hair, tanned skin, pale blue-green eyes, softly chiseled bone structure, with a bodybuilder's physique—and very well put together, in his custom fitted, steely blue designer suit. I'd assumed he was married—with kids, a house in the suburbs, and probably a dog or two.

Wow. Was I wrong. Not only was Adam not married, not saddled with kids and a suburban lifestyle, he'd never even came close to popping the question to a woman—other than the high school girlfriend that he'd ditched in law school. And his profession, as the top divorce attorney in Beverley Hills and the entire LA

County alike, had done nothing to sell him on the institution of marriage, or relationships in general.

I, myself, had just ended a somewhat long relationship; that I wouldn't say was serious, at least not as it should have been for living together for six months. This was just another in a series of failed relationships for me—further disheartening me of the male gender as a whole and their lack of evolvement when it came to a successful business woman, and convincing me that I was meant to live alone, without a traditional partner to share my life with.

Adam and I ended up sharing the night together and experiencing, what I would say was, the best sex of my life.

It wasn't until a week later that I heard from Adam again. I avoided his first two calls—unsure how he'd even found me or obtained my number. But when I opened the package he'd sent over, and saw a single pair of handcuffs, I must say, I was enticed; at least enough to return his call and see what he had in mind.

As if the handcuffs hadn't alluded to that...

Note From the Author

Thank you for purchasing 'First Sight: The Deal Prequel.' I hope you enjoyed reading Adam and Bethany's story, as much as I loved writing about them. Lizzy's story will be next, so keep your eyes open.

Following are links to my other books, and Chapter One excerpt from my adult contemporary romance, 'Memory Betrayal.'

If you have a second, please consider leaving a review on Amazon.com. Goodreads.com, or point of sale. I'd love to hear from you.☺

Thank you again,
Deborah Ann

And you can follow me on:

My Website ~ http://www.DeborahAnnAuthor.com
Author Central ~ http://www.amazon.com/DeborahAnn/e/B009QQK471/
Goodreads ~ https://www.goodreads.com/author/show/6023652.Deborah_Ann
Facebook ~ https://www.facebook.com/deborah.ann.9212
Fan Pages ~ https://www.facebook.com/pages/Destiny/461854110519696
https://www.facebook.com/pages/Deborah-Ann/164045733793955
Twitter ~ https://twitter.com/DeborahAnn11
Pinterest ~ http://www.pinterest.com/deborahanndesti/
Instagram ~ https://instagram.com/DeborahAnnAuthor/

Deborah Ann

Other Books ~
    The Destiny Series ~ Young Adult Romance with a paranormal twist ~
        Destiny ~ book one
            Fate's Path ~ book two
    Memory Betrayal ~ Adult Contemporary Romance
    The Deal ~ Adult Contemporary Romance
Amazon links
http://www.amazon.com/Destiny-Book-One-Deborah-Ann-ebook/dp/B009HTFDOW/
http://www.amazon.com/Fates-Path-Destiny-Series-Book-ebook/dp/B00CKIOI12/
http://www.amazon.com/Memory-Betrayal-Series-Book-ebook/dp/B00FROL8B8/

http://www.amazon.com/Deal-Deborah-Ann-ebook/dp/B00PLZRB31

Print versions also available, on Amazon.com
http://www.amazon.com/Deborah-Ann/e/B009QQK471/

UK Site
http://www.amazon.co.uk/gp/product/B00FROL8B8

~ 88 ~

Memory Betrayal

~ Book One~

Deborah Ann

Brief Synopsis ~

Memory Betrayal is the story of college student Elliana Brandt and her twist of fate journey with wealthy CEO Grayson Dane.

Elliana Brandt avoids men like Grayson Dane as one would the plague.

Womanizer Grayson Dane has never met a woman he didn't like, or that he couldn't have.

So when a chance meeting brings him to her rescue and disinterested Elliana simply thanks him afterwards and leaves, stunned Grayson goes out after her, snatches her from the sidewalk before she can hail a cab, and forces her into his Escalade, unaware of the tragedy he was about to inflict on her, or that he'd wake up in a hospital bed, her at his side, with everyone under the impression that she is his wife. Including Elliana herself.

The ball was already rolling, what could he do...?

Chapter One ~ Excerpt

"Smells like '*sex on the Beach*,'" Grayson Dane quipped over the lively crowd and loud music, flirtatiously staring to the angelic beauty before him.

One delicate, dark brow arched above Elliana Brandt's wide, violet eyes. "Excuse me?!" *Certainly she did not hear the attractive man's remark correctly.*

Mr. Dane looked to the beauty with wicked amusement. "The drink…soaking your dress?" He gestured to the front of her dress, his gray eyes raking over her body: her pale lavender, cocktail soaked dress clinging to the front of her, leaving little to Grayson's imagination. He knew it was inappropriate to be ogling her like he was, but he couldn't stop himself, the young woman was beautiful, innocently so.

A flash of heat reared under Elliana's skin. She hated these things, almost as much as she hated these places and the men who frequented them. But Kat was her closest friend, her roommate, and as maid of honor it was Elli's required duty to show the bride-to-be one last, single 'girls gone wild' night out. That was how she came to be so unfathomably, unbearably uncomfortable, fleeing to the restroom for a reprieve. But as luck would have it, more discomfort and humiliation was hurled upon Elli, when a lecherous drunk standing at the bar grabbed hold of her en route, his groping hands feeling her backside and squeezing her rear. In Elli's frantic attempt to free herself, she swung with great momentum, her flattened palm connecting solid with the handsy drunk's temple, stunning him. Abruptly released from his clutches, Elli was sent careening, smashing into a tipsy, two fisted drink toting girl passing by, dousing Elli with the drinks she was carrying. The colorfully tattooed and pierced girl angrily spewed out a string of profanity, spectacularly cursing Elli out before moving on. It was more than Elli could take; her eyes welled with tears, frozen in place looking to her soaked and ruined, syrup covered dress, when the attractive man with the clever drink remark stole her attention.

Elli blinked back her well of tears, her voice shaky, "Is that supposed to be funny?"

Shit! Tears! You're an ass Grayson, making an angel cry. "No...that was in poor taste. I apologize." His hand tenderly touched her arm as he moved closer, taking pity on her. "Let me help you." He grabbed the nearest cocktail waitress, pressing her for towels.

"Thank you," Elli spoke faintly, an appreciative smile warming her features.

Christ, even her voice is angelic, Grayson thought, shrugging from his suit jacket. He swung the much too large jacket over the angel's shoulders, tugging with reluctance at the lapel, making sure to cover the front of her. He was sorry to see the soaked dress and the revealings of her body shielded, but he certainly didn't want to share that view with anyone else. Grayson wanted to keep it, *and her*, his alone.

Thank God that beautiful image was so vividly burned in my memory.

Elli blushed, her tentative, violet eyes peering up to him through her long, dark lashes, noticing now how truly gorgeous the man was: shimmery blond hair, sensual gray eyes, flawless tanned skin, strong jawline, magnificent bone structure, and tall —the perfect height, not towering over her but big enough to comfortably fit within his arms, secure beneath his broad shoulders, and rest her head on his chest.

Grayson gave her a heart melting smile, reaching his arm around her shoulders and tucking her in close—as if he'd just heard her thoughts. He turned his head back, glaring at the drunken bastard seated at the bar. *Yeah, that's right asshole, you're lucky the angel needs my help, otherwise my fist would be rearranging your slimy face right now, making her smack upside your head feel like a love tap.*

Grayson led Elli to his private table, right away seating her in a chair. He grabbed the damp towel, leaving the dry ones on the table.

Elli, in some sort of shock up until now, finally found her voice again when she saw the good-looking man gesturing toward her neck with the towel. "I can do that," she asserted.

"Nonsense, you are unable to see the area." *Not to mention, if I let you do it yourself, then I would be unable to enjoy the wiles of your beauty myself, and delight in being close to you.* He smoothed the cool, damp towel over her neck, gently removing the sticky spirits from her skin. *Definitely 'Sex on the Beach,' I would know that scent anywhere.*

Holy crap, Elli thought, struck with another flash of heat. *Can skin catch fire...? Spontaneously burst into flames and combust, maybe?*

Grayson noticed the flush of the angel's skin and haughtily grinned. He was getting to her, just as he did most women. She would be unable to resist the effects of his charm, he knew, and soon be his.

"I am quite certain you are an angel, but even an angel such as yourself must have a name?"

Elli gulped, the towel rubbing between the open V-neck of her dress. Her heart sped up beneath his touch, at the same moment catching the scent of the spilled drinks. The attractive man was right, '*Sex on the Beach*,' she'd know that fruity, sweet scent anywhere—her drink of choice when she entered college, until indulging in several too many and puking them up for the remainder of the evening; no, she'd likely never forget that smell.

"Name...?" he prompted, looking to her expectantly with a delicious smile.

Whoa! Elli's lashes fluttered, "Eh...Elliana."

"Elliana—" her name seductively rolled off his tongue, "a lovely name, for a lovely angel." He reached to her hand, tenderly holding it as he raised her arm and slid the towel along. "And do you have a last name, Elliana...?"

Not so fast, Mr. Sauvé. "Elliana will do."

A fascinated smile presented itself on Mr. Dane's face. *As it should be, I must earn that right.* "Well, Elliana, I am Grayson Dane. It is my pleasure to make your acquaintance." His fingertips flirtatiously tickled across Elli's palm, grazing something cold and hard on the way to her fingers. *Shit!* He glanced to her hand, a sickened feeling striking his gut.

"You're married?"

"No," Elli murmured. "It was my mother's."

Was?! "And do you wear the ring as a deterrent—because it could be?"

"I wear it as a reminder—a vow." She slipped her hand from Grayson's, her eyes turning down.

Grayson wanted to ask about the vow, but with the way Elliana withdrew, he'd visibly touched on an upsetting subject. He'd assumed the angel was alone, for only single girls looking to hook up came to The 207 Lounge. This club is known for it. An incredibly stupid assumption; of course a woman this beautiful is not here alone. Truthfully, she is of a higher class than the usual, uh, *clientele* of women. Her reaction to the groping drunk at the bar was proof of that.

What kind of idiot would bring his girl here? Only a complete jackass, that's who.

"Where is your date, Elliana?"

Elli's surprised eyes swung to Grayson, taken back by the somewhat harsh tone in which he spoke. "That would be the one with the veil, on stage, singing poorly with the band." She innocently smiled.

Grayson chuckled with relief. "Bachelorette party, huh?"

"She is the only one who could get me to enter a club like this," Elliana divulged. "I don't usually frequent such places. They make my skin crawl."

Of course they do. She is too angelic for the meat market, and clearly doesn't belong—as I thought.

Grayson reached behind Elliana, tossing the soiled towel on the table and sweeping a clean one into his hand. He handed the towel to Elli. "For your legs," he said. "Though, I would be happy to clean them for you as well." A mischievous grin marked his features.

Yeah, I bet you would. Elli nervously gnawed on her bottom lip, the flash of heat again burning under her skin.

Grayson tenderly slipped his finger along the inside of her lip, freeing it from under her teeth. "That takes away from your beauty," he murmured.

Holy crap! Elliana's lip sparked from his touch, her insides tugging as the sweet taste of his skin, mixed with the fruity drink remains, burst in her mouth. She dropped the towel.

Grayson Dane's gray eyes smoldered in their look to her. "I'd very much like to dance with you."

Elli's breath caught. *Impossible! My skin is sure to burst into flames at that. I need to get away from this guy.* She steadied her heart.

"Thank you. But I should be getting home to change." *And salvage my dress.*

The good-looking man was taken aback by the words the angel spoke; rejection was a thing Grayson Dane was unaccustomed to.

Hmm… We'll see about that.

Grayson's one leg moved between Elli's knees as he leaned, his hands clutching the table on either side of her. "I was really hoping I could get you to dance with me," he whispered, his cheek lightly touching to Elli's while his lips met her ear. "You are nicely covered by my jacket, thus no need to change. And I promise to protect you from the advances of other men."

And who will protect me from you?

"It is not other men I fear now," Elli breathed.

Ahh…As it should be, Grayson thought. He pressed a hand to Elli's back, peeling her from the chair as he straightened upright. He was greatly looking forward to holding the angel close. And as luck would have it, a slow song resounded through the club, all but clearing the dance floor. *People don't come here for romantic slow dances, it's more of a bump and grind kind of place.*

"I am not a very good dancer. You will be sorely disappointed."

"Fortunate for you, I am a superb dancer." His lips curled into a wickedly seductive grin.

Elli swallowed hard, her pulse quickening.

Grayson Dane tucked Elliana into his side as he led her ahead, sure to protect his delicate angel as promised. He stopped in the center of the low-lit dance floor, the murmured reflection of colored lights casting a kaleidoscopic glow over their features.

Elli began to tremble when Grayson moved to unbutton the jacket she was wearing—*his jacket*. She flinched and pulled back. But Grayson held her fast.

"Relax, beautiful angel...I said I'd protect you. I just want to be able to feel your closeness."

Holy Mother of Christ.

Elli felt her ragged breath, her insides alerting her to run from this man, but her feet unyielding, uncooperative. She instead focused on Grayson's soothing gray eyes as she felt the jacket open up and Grayson's arm slip inside, snaking around her back and pulling her to press against the front of him.

"That's better," he murmured into her hair—the delights of *jasmine* indulging his senses—his other hand clutching hers and holding it preciously to him as he swayed with Elliana on the dance floor.

The fire beneath Elliana's skin extinguished, and her jagged breath calmed to a smooth rhythm, feeling complete serenity in Grayson Dane's arms.

Elli's nearly closed eyelids suddenly flew open, catching sight of Kat at the edge of the dance floor, giving her a quizzical look. Elli immediately pulled back, distancing herself from Grayson.

Shit, I'm losing her, thought Grayson, feeling the angel tense in his arms. He slid his hand to the small of her back, affectionately rubbing his thumb back and forth, and inadvertently feeling the likes of her intimates underneath: a lacy triangle, he could imagine the thin strings of lace attached and the parts of her that they hugged.

"Nice," Kat mouthed, "Armani." Elli assumed she meant the jacket—Katrina is fluent in all things designer. She gestured the tugging of lapels, *"And hot,"* Kat added, just before Elliana turned her gaze away.

"Everything all right?" Grayson asked her, showing a dangerous smile, sure to melt her.

"It's time I go."

"Aren't you enjoying yourself with me?" He sounded like a wounded little boy. "I am quite enjoying myself with you."

Oh my. "It's not that." Elli's violet eyes looked up coyly through her fluttering dark lashes, meeting the sparking gray of Grayson's.

"Then let me take you. I will be a perfect gentleman."

Right. "I don't take rides from strangers."

"I am hardly a stranger at this point." The words floated past his lips in a hypnotic swirl, nearly entrancing Elli beyond response.

She closed her eyes and took a deep breath, clearing Grayson's magical charm from her head. "I…uh…came with friends, and I need to leave with those friends. But thank you for your kindness …and your help." Elli shrugged from Grayson Dane's jacket and handed it back to him. "And thank you for the use of your jacket."

Though quite stunned, Grayson caught her wrist as she stepped off.

Elliana's eyes swung to him, a severe, blatant warning. "You need to let me go!"

What's wrong with this girl, she can't get away from me quick enough. I've never had this response before.

Grayson respectfully, but reluctantly, let loose of his angel, watching as she bolted to her friends with an unfamiliar feeling coming over him.

Kat's grin was like a beaming force, lighting Elli's way to her. *Oh no, I know that look, relentless Kat!* "Spill it…that guy is gorgeous…of godly proportions gorgeous!" Kat's words assaulted Elli as she approached her.

Elli blushed, nervously biting at her bottom lip, the action quickly reminding her of Grayson's earlier reaction to her nervous gnawing of her bottom lip, the spark of his touch, and the taste of his skin. Elli blushed harder, her breath erratic. "There's nothing to say."

Are you kidding me? Thought Kat. *The flush of your skin, clamming up, that says it all, my dear friend.* "At least tell me his name?" *I assume it's not Mr. Armani, or Gorgeous God.*

"It doesn't matter," Elli said determinedly. "I'm never going to see him again."

"I'm not so sure of that," Kat quipped. "I saw the way he looked at you…you got under his skin. As I think he did yours."

Elli gave her a curious look. "I'm not going to let some strange guy, no matter how good-looking he is, pick me up in a bar."

Kat gazed back at her with an expression of empathy now. "You have to let someone in, Elli; it's been five years. You can't continue to let the past destroy your future." She touched a compassionate hand on Elli's wrist. "He looked decent. I am not saying go home with him, maybe a date. At least give him your phone number."

Elli felt it best not to mention how her skin nearly erupted in flames in the man's presence.

Meanwhile, Grayson Dane was in a state of insurmountable twisting. Women don't pass him up...*Ever*...which made him want Elliana that much more.

The angel is different—as I first felt.

In an attempt to draw her back, Grayson cleverly sent Elliana a drink.

It would at least keep me in her thoughts, he figured.

Grayson observed Elliana from his table across the room, a luminescent, angelic glow surrounding her and causing her to stand out amongst the rest.

A scantily clad cocktail waitress with ruby red lips, heavily charcoal lined cat eyes, and a ratted nest of hair—straw-colored, that looked straight from the fifties—slinked up beside Elliana, all but blocking Grayson's view. She was holding the tray with Elliana's drink, but made no physical attempt to give it to her, not that Grayson could see anyway. She appeared to be conversing with Elliana...

Katrina's eyebrows rose, "'*Sex on the Beach*?!'" she said in reference of the lone drink on the waitress's tray. "That's a gesture if I ever saw one."

Elli rolled her eyes, fighting back her urge to smile. *He is determined, if nothing else.* "Tell the gentleman thank you, but I'm not interested in his '*Sex on the Beach*.'"

The waitress appeared incredulous. "Are you sure?" She turned to face Grayson's direction. "Look at him, honey. You don't say no to a man like that!"

Elli averted glancing toward Grayson—she already felt the heat of his gaze on her—but Kat and the rest of the party took full advantage of the opportunity to gawk at him.

Grayson gave a polite wave and flashed the ladies an award winning smile, relishing in the moment. *Now these women know how to respond to a man*, he thought smugly.

"His friend's not bad either," Katrina remarked.

Friend?! Elli's head shot Grayson's direction in reaction, before she thought not to. *I assumed he was alone, in want of a pick-up and a quick exit.* Her breath caught at Grayson's stare, hardly noticing the handsome friend at his side. Elliana wanted very badly to turn away and draw her eyes from Grayson's wanting stare, afraid her eyes might also flame.

"You don't turn a man like that down," the waitress repeated.

"Let him in!" Kat pushed.

Elli drew in a deep breath, rescinding her eyes from Grayson's wanting stare, her focus now determinedly back on the waitress. "Please pass my message on to the gentleman, and return his drink to him."

The waitress spun on her heels, shaking her head in disbelief.

Maybe he'll share his 'Sex on the Beach' with her! She is certainly less inclined to turn him down. My heart, on the other hand, can't take a man like that. He would ruin me.

Grayson watched the waitress step away from Elliana, the drink still in place.

Christ…what's it going to take? That usually works. He ran an anxious hand through his hair. *I'm not leaving without the angel. Or at least her number*, he determined.

Kat suddenly caught sight of Elli's dress. *That's why she was wearing the God's jacket*, she realized. "What happened to your dress?"

"Long story—it is because of that that I need to go."

"It's almost closing time anyway. And Rodger texted me a bit ago and said that Booker passed out." She rolled her eyes dramatically. "He is such a wuss when it comes to drinking. We'll have to pick him up on our way home."

"You stay for the last hour," Elli urged her friend. "Or, even stay the night upstairs in the hotel suite with the rest of the girls. I can take a cab and see to it that your overindulged fiancé makes it home safely."

Kat's hands sat on her hips. "You're sure? Because I'm fairly certain that overindulged fiancés are not a responsibility of the maid of honor—Leave it to you to over excel at that, too!"

Elliana smiled, giving a kind hug to her friend before she made her escape, an escape she hoped would evade notice from the persistent and good-looking, skin fire starting, Mr. Dane…

~ * ~

Share Elliana and Grayson's story of unexpected love, betrayal, heartbreak, past secrets, and healing.

'Memory Betrayal' is full novel length, 450 print pages.
http://www.amazon.com/Memory-Betrayal-Series-Book-ebook/dp/
B00FROL8B8/
http://www.amazon.com/Deborah-Ann/e/B009QQK471/

In addition to 'The Deal' and 'The Memory Betrayal Series' Deborah Ann is the Author of 'The Destiny Series,' a Young Adult Romance Series.

Destiny

~ Book One ~

Deborah Ann

Danielle Kennedy is not one to believe in fairy tale love or destiny holding a plan for the future, nor does she believe in mythical legends, vampires, or spirits…

At sixteen, athletic, honor student Danielle has her life planned out: study hard, play soccer even harder, and slide through high school under the radar. It was a good plan, a solid plan, one that's worked so far, until Cayden Bridwell—the longtime shy and brainy classmate she has ignored—rides in on his motorcycle and obliterates her plans. Now, life as Danielle knows it, will never be the same.

Wealthy Cayden—only recently coming into his own and learning the shocking truth, that as the Seventh Son of a Seventh Son, he is the chosen one, gifted with powers—has shyly stood back and watched unassuming and unsuspecting Danielle, grow into the beautiful girl she is, knowing all along of their destiny to be together, and waiting for the time to be right. After his rapid growth spurt and realizing his full powers and strength, that time is now! Cayden is intent on winning her heart.

But the euphoria of their intoxicating attraction is soon shadowed by despair; neither are prepared for the danger that will ensue, the lives that will be at risk, or the secrets they will be forced to keep, when they discover that destiny's gifts come with a curse, opening their world to nightmares that become reality and mythical legends that become real, with immortal beings seeking to sway Cayden to the dark side to steal his eternal soul and powers—including Danielle, as his destined soul mate...

Destiny is a sweet and intoxicating fairy tale romance with a paranormal twist, and the first book in the Destiny series.

Come fall in love with Danielle and Cayden, as they discover the power and passion of an all-consuming first love, and fight to protect each other and the life they were destined for...

http://www.amazon.com/Destiny-Book-One-Deborah-Ann-ebook/dp/ B009HTFDOW/

Also Available

The Destiny Series

~ Book Two ~

Fate's Path

When fate's curse sweeps upon Danielle and Cayden, the secrets behind their destiny begin to be revealed...

Will they be able to fight the darkness seeping in and swaying them, or give in to the power and passion of their all-consuming love, risking Cayden's pure soul and crossing them to the dark side...?

http://www.amazon.com/Fates-Path-Destiny-Series-Book-ebook/dp/B00CKIOI12/

For longer previews of each book, follow links to Amazon.com, or sample on Kindle.

http://www.amazon.com/Deborah-Ann/e/B009QQK47I/

About The Author

~

Deborah Ann lives in Northern California with her husband and their two children, where she has enjoyed a long career in the Beauty Industry.

After years of reading with her children and passing on a love for books, Deborah was inspired to write the Destiny Series. What started out in the beginning, as a celebration of a loving, young, innocent friendship and the affecting separation after a move, spun into a mythical journey of the loving binds of friendship, deep family ties, and an intoxicating fairy tale romance, with the power of love that knows no bounds.

'Memory Betrayal' & 'The Deal' followed, with a leap from young adult romance, to adult romance. And while it can be a balancing act at times, Deborah sneaks in as much time as she can to slip into the lives of her characters, and the magical world in which they live...

Deborah Ann

www.ingramcontent.com/pod-product-compliance
Lightning Source LLC
Chambersburg PA
CBHW030641130626
46552CB00002B/968